Crackaroo

GARY LEE VINCENT

Burning Bulb
PUBLISHING

Crackaroo
By **Gary Lee Vincent**

Burning Bulb Publishing
P.O. Box 4721
Bridgeport, WV 26330-4721
United States of America
www.BurningBulbPublishing.com

Cover designed by Max Cave as a work for hire for Gary Lee Vincent and Burning Bulb Publishing.

First Edition.

Paperback Edition ISBN: 978-1-964172-19-4

Also by Gary Lee Vincent

Novels
PASSAGEWAY
BELLY TIMBER
ATTACK OF THE MELONHEADS
WHEN THE BEDPOSTS SHAKE (RING OF THE SUCCUBUS)
IMPOUND
STRANGE FRIENDS
THE BEST ACTORS THAT EVER LIVED
JEROME
THE BLIND MELODY

Darkened—The West Virginia Vampire Series
DARKENED HILLS
DARKENED HOLLOWS
DARKENED WATERS
DARKENED SOULS
DARKENED MINDS
DARKENED DESTINIES

The Douglas River Vampire Series
RIVER: A VAMPIRE'S NIGHTMARE
ICARUS

The Crackimals Series
CRACKCOON
CRACKODILE
CRACKSQUATCH
CRACKROACHES
CRACKADILLO
CRACKAROO

Dedicated to
Michael Ochotorena

CHAPTER 1

It was late in the evening that summer Friday at the Sleepaway Campground on the outskirts of Buckhannon, West Virginia, when forest ranger Gary Bentley saw the two men.

The men were standing and chatting in the Sleepaway Campground parking lot.

Gary, who'd been patrolling the other side of the Tygart Valley River, which flowed right through the Sleepaway Campground, clearly couldn't hear what the men were talking about. They were also too distant for him to see their faces. It didn't matter. So long as they weren't littering or starting forest fires, or doing anything illegal, it was none of his business.

After watching the two men for a while, Gary looked away from them again and continued his inspection of the campground and its facilities. He now focused his attention on the side wall of one of the cabins, on which some kid (delinquency generally had a fixed age bracket) had spray-painted: "I like weed, you like weed, let's all smoke weed!"

Typical pothead logic, Gary thought angrily. *Now, someone's going to have to paint over that. At least I don't have to do it.*

He calmed down and even managed to laugh at the silly graffiti.

He continued back toward the bridge that connected to the parking lot. He was done with his shift now and was on his way back home. Other than for that graffiti, everything had gone smoothly today. Tonight, he planned to kick up his feet and relax in the company of his wife, Charlotte.

While Gary was crossing the bridge and staring down into the river, trying to catch sight of a catfish or trout, he heard the sound of cars starting up in the parking lot. Now, he once more remembered the two men he'd seen conversing.

He looked that way again. Two vehicles were leaving the parking lot, meaning the men hadn't arrived together. The lead car was already out of the parking lot and driving off. The other vehicle, a yellow pickup truck, was just pulling out of parking, and although Gary didn't see the face of its driver even now, he noticed it was a company vehicle. Printed boldly on the pickup truck's side amidst illustrations of monkeys, clowns, and lions, was the legend "Madam Vega's Traveling Show."

Gary smiled at the thought of old-style entertainment.

So, the circus is in town, he thought. *Haven't been to one in ages. Maybe I'll even take Charlotte. She likes that sort of family entertainment. I'll suggest it to her tonight.*

With that pleasant thought in mind, Gary stepped off the bridge and walked over to where his ranger truck was parked alongside several other vehicles.

The sky had begun darkening now, and this evening's wind seemed a little cool for camping, but Gary smiled. He was an outdoors person and relished both the job he did and the environment he worked in. Some folks might claim he lacked ambition. He just saw it as him being himself.

I'm blessed for sure, he thought happily, as he stepped around the rear of his truck to reach the driver's door. *I'm one of those fortunate people who are able to spend their lives doing what they love. I love working as a forest ranger; I really do!*

Then, before he completed the turn to reach the truck's door, Gary Bentley spotted something on the floor of the parking lot and his brow clouded over.

Hey, what's that? he asked himself and walked over to pick it up.

Oh, no no no no no! Gary thought on recognizing what he'd picked up. It was a small orange 'candy,' marshmallow-like in that it had a slight powdery covering. He licked it and winced at its bitter taste.

Agent Orange, he thought in disgust, spitting what he'd tasted onto the floor. To Gary's mind, Agent Orange was the worst narcotic ever conceived. A plague that deserved to be eliminated, but which West Virginian law enforcement were seemingly powerless to completely wipe out, though strangely (and thankfully, to Gary's thinking), so far the drug hadn't yet spread much further than the Mountain State.

Agent Orange is the evil gift that simply refuses to stop giving.

Gary's previously pleasant day had now completely nosedived.

But how did this chunk of orange get here? he wondered. *It ain't like it's got legs and walked from town up into the mountains. Hmmm*

Then he remembered the two men he'd earlier seen chatting. There hadn't seemed to be anything furtive about their conversation, but there might have been.

Drug dealers love to transact their business in out-of-the-way places like this. So, did those two guys bring the stuff out here? That seems quite possible. One of those vehicles—yeah, the circus one—was parked right where I'm standing now, right where I found the orange. And of course, circuses tend to have animals in them, and animals and Agent Orange don't mix well in the least. In fact, I'd rather have a human addicted to Agent Orange than an animal in the same condition.

But he knew he might be wrong. *It may just be damn junkie campers again. This wouldn't be the first time someone's brought Agent Orange here to get high. I really wish the junkies would take their addiction to another campground.*

Gary Bentley put the piece of Agent Orange away in his shirt pocket. *At least I got the name of that circus, just in case. I hope that I'm wrong and it's really some orangehead kid that's lost a chunk of his addiction on the parking lot floor. Hopefully, he won't think his girlfriend stole it and bash her head in.*

Wincing at that thought, Gary Bentley got into his ranger truck, backed out of the parking lot, and headed out of the campground.

He tried to keep things in perspective. The day hadn't been ruined. There was simply a possibility of trouble, but no point in worrying about it.If Gary Bentley had had any idea what would soon happen around him, he'd have run screaming to a shrink.

CHAPTER 2

"Oh yes, darling, I'd love to go see Madam Vega's Traveling Show," Charlotte Bentley said enthusiastically once Gary told her about it. "I saw an ad for them online, and when I checked the reviews, they were all very good."

Gary nodded grimly. "That's all well and good, hon, but now, we ain't just going there for the fun and games."

"What are you talking about, darling?" Charlotte asked.

It was after dinnertime, and husband and wife were seated comfortably on their living room couch watching TV. Normally, they had a war over who controlled the remote control. Tonight, however, Gary was so distracted that he didn't complain when Charlotte snared the TV remote for herself and switched to a romantic sitcom.

Gary got out the chunk of Agent Orange that he'd been carrying around all day. "*This* is the problem," he explained to his wife. "I found *this* in the parking lot on my way back home."

Charlotte stared at the drug in surprise. "Doesn't our state ever run out of this stuff?"

"Beats me," Gary replied. "All I know is . . . each time I find chunks of this somewhere, there's a darn thunderstorm on the horizon."

Charlotte nodded. "Yes, sweetheart, I know that. What I don't understand is how it connects to the circus that's in town this week."

So, with TV romance forgotten for the moment, Gary Bentley explained to his wife about the two men he'd seen talking in the campground parking lot before he'd discovered the drug there, and the circus pickup truck he'd seen leaving there.

"Oh, so you think . . ."

Gary nodded. "Of course, I'm just clutching at straws here, but better safe than sorry, like they say."

He pointed at Charlotte's phone, which sat on the end table beside her. "Honey, see if you can book us tickets to Madam Vega's for one of this weekend's shows."

Charlotte Googled Madam Vega's up on her phone, studied the website menus for a while, and finally opened up the Tickets page.

"Saturday or Sunday?" she asked after studying the options.

"What time are the shows?"

"2 p.m. and 6 p.m. tomorrow and 3 p.m. on Sunday." She looked at him inquiringly. "Which should we book?"

"Tomorrow's my day off. Best we attend the 2 p.m. show. Then we can still head out for dinner afterward if we feel like it."

Charlotte made the booking and put her phone down again. She smiled at Gary. "Now try to relax, honey. Maybe what happened is simply that other scenario you suggested. You know, a drug addict losing part of his supply."

Gary sighed. "I'd love to believe that. I really would. But once I see that Agent Orange stuff anywhere, it's like I'm once more back in one of those nasty past experiences again."

"Oh, I know, I know," Charlotte said. "But maybe this time things are different." She snuggled up close to him and laid her head on his shoulder. "So just relax, darling."

Gary tried to relax. It wasn't easy.

CHAPTER 3

Elaine Vega, the proprietress of Madam Vega's traveling circus, was an attractive blonde with long hair and green eyes. She was also a shrewd businesswoman.

Elaine had inherited the circus from her late husband, Larry. In addition to owning and running the circus, Larry Vega had been a strongman. From being a USA Olympic Team champion weightlifter, Larry had graduated to lifting people and animals on his shoulders and performing other feats of strength under the Big Top.

That was until the day that a scorpion stung him on the ankle while he was practicing carrying a riding pony around the ring.

The scorpion's sting hadn't killed Larry. Well, not directly. But it weakened him so that the horse fell on top of him and flattened him.

No one knew how the scorpion had gotten into the enclosure.

Anyhow . . . exit Larry as circus owner and enter Elaine.

Even when Larry had been alive, Elaine had been a mainstay of his decision-making, and so she had little difficulty handling the demands of running the business now, and more importantly, of turning a profit while doing so.

But tonight, that profit seemed in jeopardy.

***

"Honest, Elaine, I've no idea what's going on," Kevin Lagen said, scratching his head as he, Elaine, and Cedric stared into the open safe in Elaine's tent. "This is driving me crazy too. Each night after the show, I put the cash into the safe. You know the rest."

Elaine gestured to Kevin to lock up the safe again. Then she walked over to her couch and sat on it, while Kevin and Cedric both stood, waiting to hear what she'd say.

The three of them were in Elaine's camper, all around which they could hear the noises of the circus settling down for the night. Neighing horses, the lions growling while they were fed, monkeys chittering, and the random noises of the circus performers either watching TV or talking in their caravans.

Kevin Lagen was the circus's accountant, though he also doubled as one of the jugglers. Kevin had been with the circus since Elaine's late husband's days, and neither Larry then nor herself now had ever found the slightest fault with his handling of the business's finances.

If anything, he's too damn honest, she thought, turning her gaze on Cedric instead.

Cedric Williams was the circus's new strongman, and also Elaine's boyfriend. Okay, so even Elaine admitted it: She did have a thing for huge and muscular men.

Cedric wasn't exactly brainy. He had nowhere near Kevin's smarts. He was simply a good-looking blonde man, with muscles that would put a pro wrestler to shame. But he was as devoted to Elaine as she was to him. Which was a lot.

"What do you think is going on here, Cedric?" Elaine asked him in a helpless voice. "Who's been stealing our money? If this keeps up, by the month's end, we're gonna be short on salaries."

Yes, someone had been stealing money from Elaine's safe, which, in all honesty, wasn't the safest safe in West Virginia. The safe was an old and rickety thing from perhaps the 1930s, which Elaine still kept because it held sentimental value for her.

"Someday, someone's gonna start stealing from in there and you're gonna regret not upgrading to a new model," Cedric had told Elaine on more than one occasion.

And right now, she did regret not listening to him. So far, they'd lost three thousand dollars this week—most of the gate takings. Thankfully, most of the circus's visitors had booked their tickets online, or else the disaster would be even bigger. Elaine ran a large operation and couldn't afford to lose money like this.

"Alright, let's think this through," Cedric said, scratching his ear with a muscular finger. "Kev puts the cash in the safe every night, like he normally does, but the money only vanished on Wednesday and tonight."

Kevin gestured to the pile of cash that lay on a counter in the camper. "And of course, the money that vanishes is the previous days' gate takings, because we only open up the safe at night to put in the new take."

Elaine and Cedric nodded to this. "What are you getting at?" Cedric asked.

Kevin raised a finger and wagged it at them. "Well, on Wednesday, we were over in Morgantown, and this weekend, we're here in Buckhannon. And considering that both towns are quite distant from each other, what does that immediately suggest to you?"

Elaine thought she saw what he meant. "You're trying to say the thief couldn't have been following us around, aren't you?"

"Exactly," Kevin Lagen agreed. "So, to state the obvious, this is clearly an inside job." He nodded at his two companions. "One of our own people is breaking in here and stealing our money."

"Any suspects?" Elaine asked. "Kev, you've had several days to think this over. You must have someone who you think could be doing this to me . . . to all of us."

Kevin shook his head. "I don't, Elaine. The problem is, I can't figure out who could possibly know the safe's combination other than yourself and Cedric." He shrugged at them both. "Yeah, I know, it's a puzzling puzzle. What I suggest, however, is that we stop keeping the cash in there from henceforth."

Elaine sighed. "Yeah, yeah, I know. You suggested putting the money elsewhere after the first time. But back then, I thought the thief was a freaking local, and this wouldn't happen again. How fucking wrong I was."

Cedric walked over to her side and slipped his arm around her. "Now, don't start blaming yourself, baby. I, too, thought the thief was some guy from Morgantown."

He nodded at Kevin. "I think you'd better hold onto the money from now on. At least until we catch the thief."

Kevin looked at Elaine for confirmation of this.

She nodded back. "Yeah, do like Cedric says. Keep the cash with you." She frowned. "And in the meantime, we'll all keep our eyes peeled and watch to see who is stealing our money."

"And then we'll feed them to the lions," Cedric said.

"Yeah, we will, baby," Elaine agreed and then burst out laughing. "It'll save us quite a lot of money."

"You're both not serious, are you?" Kevin asked, a little nervously.

"Wait and see, man," Cedric said. "Just you wait and see."

Kevin nodded and quickly gathered up tonight's gate takings. "Well, if you don't need me anymore tonight, I'll best get back to my tent. I wanna get some rest before our two shows tomorrow."

"See you," Elaine waved as he left. When he opened the door, she could see down between the campers to the end of Buck's Field where the circus was being held this week. Before Kevin swung the camper door closed, Elaine caught a glimpse of Ronald the kangaroo trainer and his charge Sydney. The kangaroo was hopping obediently after Ronald; both figures trailed by long shadows in the moonlight.

The door closed, cutting off her view of the outside world, and she turned back to Cedric.

"Did you see how nervous Kev was?" Cedric asked. "You don't think he stole the cash, do you?"

Elaine shook her head. "Not Kev. He'd never steal from us. He was just frightened, 'cos he thought we were serious about throwing the thief to the lions when we caught him. You know that's murder."

Cedric laughed. "Can't the guy take a joke?"

Elaine sighed. "I really do wish we could throw the thief to the lions. It would save us quite a lot of money in animal feed, especially as compensation for what the asshole's stolen."

CHAPTER 4

The next afternoon, Gary and Charlotte drove over to the circus as planned.

Even approaching from a distance, husband and wife could both make out the giant blue marquee of the Big Top with MADAM VEGA'S TRAVELING SHOW boldly printed on it in yellow.

Then, as they turned off the highway and were facing the circus venue, they were swamped with the cars of other attendees for the afternoon show.

"It's been ages since I last saw something like this," Charlotte said in an excited voice. "I hope they have lots of clowns."

Gary grunted. Tormented by dreams of killer clowns on crack, he'd been unable to sleep well last night.

They arrived, and a clown on stilts waved them over to an area of the parking lot. Gary parked, and they both alighted. Once out of the car and standing in the aura of the circus, Gary found it hard to remain grim. The circus venue was a huge field, with just the countryside nearby, and seeing as Gary loved the open air, this place was like a dream come true. Yeah, there were lots of people milling about, getting in and out of their cars, and laughing, but the simple freedom of the big open space all around and the open sky above was priceless.

Gary and Charlotte walked past a wire-fenced enclosure with a kangaroo in it. The animal was looking out at the arriving people as if delighted to see them, too.

Charlotte waved at the kangaroo. It leaned back and seemed to peer so suspiciously at her that she burst out laughing.

"Hey, Sydney, over here!" a man on the opposite side of the enclosure called out, and the kangaroo hopped away from the fence and toward him.

Gary and Charlotte stopped at a concession stall and bought drinks and cotton candy.

"We've still ten minutes before the show starts," Charlotte told Gary. "Let's walk around for a while before we look for our seats."

"Sure, honey," Gary agreed. He had no objections to wandering the circus grounds. He had no plan, either; he just intended to hang around here and get a feel of the place, if he could. He didn't pride himself on having the instincts of a policeman when it came to crime-busting, but he felt sure he'd notice if anything was glaringly wrong.

They strolled through the circus grounds and through the gathering crowd, till they reached the circus's farther limits and then they turned back. By then everyone was hurrying inside the Big Top tent.

"Okay, let's have our seats," Gary said, and he and Charlotte followed the crowd inside.

CHAPTER 5

No doubt about it; the show was fun. The aerial acrobatics, the jugglers and clowns, the horse riding stunts and the animal acts, particularly the monkeys, kept the audience thoroughly entertained.

Gary did have a moment's fear however when the lion tamer put his head into the lion's mouth. He always felt this way when he saw this act. Though he knew the lion wouldn't hurt the man, willingly putting your head into a lion's mouth had always struck him a very foolhardy thing to do.

Charlotte of course, was goggle-eyed at the act, eating cotton candy, and 'oohing' and 'aahing' with everyone else. Charlotte loved animals, especially wild animals, and so was having the time of her life right now.

Gary nudged her with his elbow. "What I wanna know," he whispered, "is what happens if a bee or a wasp suddenly stings that lion on the ass?"

"I never actually thought of that," Charlotte replied. "Maybe they never do. Maybe bees and wasps are allergic to lion farts. Maybe it kills them like bug spray."

Gary burst out laughing and concentrated on the show.

The lion tamer survived today's act of intrepid stupidity.

And then the show's impresario Madam Vega was carried in, standing on the shoulders of the strongman Cedric, who'd already performed several astounding feats of strength, including standing in place while four men on motorcycles tried to get their bikes to pull him off of his feet. The four motorbikes had revved like thunder, and their wheels had spun like crazy, but the bikers had failed to accomplish their intention. And then, like the ancient titan Hercules,

Cedric had dragged each of their motorbikes to the ground, earning himself a thunderous ovation.

Now Cedric lowered Madam Vega so she was sitting on his shoulder. A showgirl passed her a microphone.

"Is everyone having a great time so far!?" she asked.

When the affirmative yells subsided, the impresario said, "Well, now, we've got a special treat for you all. Sydney, the boxing kangaroo."

And to resounding applause, Sydney hopped into the ring. The kangaroo was the same one they'd seen outside, only now it was wearing a set of red boxing gloves.

"I didn't know they still had kangaroo boxing events," Charlotte whispered. "Aren't they illegal?"

"I've no idea myself," Gary replied as the kangaroo stood in the middle of the ring waiting for its first opponent.

In the meantime, Cedric had carried Madam Vega to the far side of the ring.

"So, Ladies and Gentlemen, girls and boys," Madam Vega said, "Sydney is ready to fight. But whom will she fight today, I wonder? Maybe, we should select someone from the audience. Would anyone be interested in boxing our champion kangaroo!"

Several men raised their hands. Now, mingled in with the applause, there were some cheers from the audience, some who maybe imagined they were set to watch an actual, serious contest between man and animal.

But then, loud clown music erupted from the tent's concealed speakers, and a clown cartwheeled into the ring.

"Oh, sorry, gentlemen, but you're too late. It appears that Bumble, the clown, accepts Sydney's challenge.

Charlotte heaved a sigh of relief. "I thought they were actually gonna fight," she whispered aside to Gary, while Bumble the clown fumbled on his own unrealistically large boxing gloves, dropping them several times in the process, while the kangaroo bounced about impatiently like she was Muhammed Ali. "I'd have walked out if someone had actually hit that poor creature."

Gary shook his head. "Darling, that 'poor creature' of yours is extremely dangerous. The reason it's wearing gloves in this boxing contest is because it can easily claw a man's eyes out. And you'll notice Bumble is well-padded around the belly and groin, that's because kangaroos kick a lot when they fight in their natural habitat. One of those kicks can kill a man."

"I didn't know that," Charlotte said.

"Neither did I until I Googled it last night."

Bumble had now gotten his boxing gloves on, and the contest began. The boxing match was a complete farce, one of the funniest things anyone in the audience had likely ever seen, with the clown holding on for dear life half of the time, while Sydney pummeled him like crazy, then running around in circles until the kangaroo belted him again. Bumble finally pulled out a large towel and threw it over the kangaroo's head. Then he ran off for dear life.

Most of the audience, Gary included, had tears of mirth in their eyes.

"You know, maybe Bumble wasn't that much of a true contender," Madam Vega said in serious tones. "From what I heard, Bumble lost the clownweight championship last week. So now, let's bring on the current clown champion: Fumble the Clown."

Loud clown music sounded again, and Fumble the Clown stepped into the boxing arena.

Fumble was small and fat and even though he already had his boxing gloves on, his pants kept falling down. Finally, he slipped them off altogether, took a proper fighting stance in his multicolored clown shorts, and was promptly knocked unconscious by Sydney.

"Oh, my, this seems a bad day to be a clown," Madam Vega proclaimed as two clowns ran in with a stretcher and rolled Fumble onto it. Then, just as they began leaving, what should happen, but that Fumble suddenly revived.

The clowns paused their leaving. Fumble got down from the stretcher and took off his boxing gloves and handed them to the larger of the two clowns, the one holding onto the rear of the stretcher. Then he took hold of the rear handles of the stretcher in that clown's place, and he and the other clown began walking away, leaving the previous stretcher-bearer to fight in his place.

The audience was in stitches by now. Sydney had been waiting patiently all this while, but once she saw the new clown holding the gloves, she bounded at him. The clown turned and fled, but only bumped into the previous boxer, who in turn now rammed the stretcher into the back of the clown in front. All three clowns went down in a heap.

Sydney hopped over the jumbled clowns and then back again.

"And the winner today, and still Vegaland Champion, Sydney the Kangaroo!"

"That's the funniest thing I ever saw in my damn life," Gary said, as six clowns arrived with stretchers to carry off their fallen fellows. "And that's a fact."

Charlotte was laughing too, with tears in her eyes. "And to think I was gonna leave!"

And then Gary's happy mood changed. Down in the circus ring, a man had just stepped into the enclosure and was walking over to Sydney the Kangaroo.

Gary froze and nudged Charlotte. "Hey, that's him!"

She looked at him in surprise. "That's who, honey?"

He gestured down at the man was leading Sydney out of the ring, to the resounding applause of the watchers. "That's the guy I saw at the campground yesterday."

Charlotte peered down at the man, who was almost out of sight now and was additionally being blocked off by the kangaroo bouncing after him. "Are you sure? I can hardly see him." She turned and looked seriously at her husband. "Are you sure, honey? Last night you said you were far away and so didn't get a good look at him."

Gary nodded and smiled. "Yeah, hon, but that same reason is exactly why I recognized him just now—because he was so far off. The guy has a way he stands that's unmistakable."

Charlotte nodded. "Well, that's great. So, you've identified one of the people who may or may not be endangering our great state. Now, calm down and enjoy the show. The kangaroo trainer isn't about running off anywhere. We can find him whenever we want to."

Gary agreed that Charlotte had a good point. And so far, it had been a great show.

"And now, Ladies and Gents, girls and boys, introducing Otis, the Knife Thrower, and Mindy Flame!"

This act was a variation of the classic blindfolded knife-thrower act. Mindy Flame both ate and blew flames while Otis peppered the board she was tied to with darts and knives, sometimes even throwing the knives through flaming hoops she threw in the air.

Gary found this even more scary than the head-in-the-lion's-mouth stupidity.

What if the guy misses his aim, or if she panics and sets herself ablaze? he wondered.

CHAPTER 6

"Wow, that was a fantastic show," Charlotte enthused as she and Gary left the enclosure.

He nodded. "I gotta agree with you, hon. I ain't laughed that much in ages. It was all I could do at times not to fall out of my seat."

They were standing in the shadow of a marquee tent, and waiting for the crowd to disperse, so they could head for their pickup truck.

Gary was a tall man, and so he easily looked over the heads of the dispersing audience.

"Hey, it's just four o'clock," Charlotte said, "what do we do now? Head home, or maybe drive into town for some food?"

When Gary didn't reply to her query, Charlotte looked up at him. "Honey, you're not listening to me. Honey!"

Gary looked down from scanning the area. "I was looking for the kangaroo trainer guy."

Charlotte sighed. "He's probably backstage, relaxing with the others. Remember, they've another show to put on in a couple of hours."

Gary nodded. "You're right. We'd better get a move on."

They set off walking in the direction of their pickup truck.

"Hey, I forgot to buy some souvenirs," Charlotte said. "Gimme some money, honey."

Gary handed her a hundred dollars and she walked back toward the souvenir shop. The shop was crowded with people, young and old, and Gary figured she'd have a long wait before it was her turn to be served.

He returned his attention to looking around. They'd stopped close to Sydney, the Kangaroo's enclosure. Sydney was back in there, sans boxing gloves, sitting and eating a slice of watermelon. On remembering the 'boxing' match the kangaroo and clowns had staged, Gary burst out laughing.

He was still laughing when a voice said. "Hey, if ain't Gary Bentley after all these years."

He turned to see the speaker, and then grinned broadly. "Eddie? It is you, right?"

"Sure is, man!" Eddie Bush said, laughing. He and Gary shook hands and then hugged. "Wow, man, it's been like ages, like forever, since we last laid eyes on each other."

Eddie wasn't alone. Gary smiled at the woman with him, and she smiled back.

"Oh, you don't know Wanda," Eddie said. "She and I have been married for . . . how long now, sweetie?"

"Five years, Eddie," Wanda replied. "Five wonderful years." She gestured around in a vague way, then told Gary, "I saw you earlier with a woman. Where'd she go?"

"Over there." Gary pointed over at the souvenir shop where Charlotte had seemingly vanished amidst the crowd mobbing the sellers.

"You and Charlotte still together, man?" Eddie asked.

Gary nodded. "Still."

Eddie laughed. "That's what I always liked about you, man; stable as a rock. Not like me, who just had to run off and see the world. And I know you're still working that ranger job, too."

Gary nodded again. "Still doin' that, too. Wouldn't trade it for the world."

"And how's your son? Sorry, but I don't recall his name anymore."

Gary laughed. "Oh, Mike is at Penn State now studying marine biology. Hey, guys, Charlotte's finally gotten free of the souvenir shop."

They all turned toward her.

Charlotte's eyes widened when she saw Eddie Bush. "I don't believe what I'm seeing. Eddie?"

Eddie laughed and they hugged. Then Eddie introduced Charlotte to his wife Wanda.

"So, did you guys enjoy the show, too?" Charlotte asked Eddie and Wanda.

"Oh, it was fucking great!" Eddie said, then looked embarrassed. "Oh, excuse my swearing. I forgot we got ladies' present."

Charlotte and Wanda smiled. "We forgive you," Wanda said.

Gary shook his head. "Same old Eddie."

"Anyway, the show was fantastic," Wanda agreed. "I almost died laughing when the kangaroo fought the clowns."

Gary pointed over at the nearby enclosure. "Ah, the new Vegaland boxing champion has fallen asleep now."

Everyone crowded up to the wire and stared at Sydney, who really had fallen asleep.

"Hey, Eddie, what are you and Wanda doing this evening?" Gary asked.

Eddie shrugged. "Nothing, really. We were just out having some fun today. Why you askin'?"

"Well, see, Charlotte and I don't have any particular plans for this evening, so seeing as it's literally been ages since you and I last saw each other, why don't we all spend this evening together and catch up on what's been happening to each other in-between." He nodded. "I'm thinking this is as good a time as any to catch up on old times."

"Yeah," Eddie agreed. "With eight years in between our last meeting, heaven knows when next we'll run into one another."

"There's Facebook," Charlotte pointed out. "It's easy to stay in touch that way."

"Nah, that social media stuff ain't for me," Eddie retorted. "And besides, you can't get drunk together on damn Facebook!"

"Amen to that brother!" Gary agreed.

"Your place or ours?" Eddie asked.

"You guys come over to our place," Gary said. "I'm conditioned to the countryside now. I ain't really comfortable hanging out in town anymore."

So, with Gary and Charlotte leading the way, the two couples got into their respective vehicles and drove away from the circus.

CHAPTER 7

"So, how'd things go?" Eddie Bush asked his wife while they drove behind Gary and Charlotte.

"Smooth and easy, baby," Wanda Bush said. Then she reached over and squeezed Eddie's thigh. "Your friend Ronald is cool. He doesn't strike me as an orangehead tho'. When I handed him the Agent Orange, he looked at the package like it was a snake he was handling."

Eddie laughed. "Ronnie's a smart fish. Just like you and me, he doesn't ever touch orange. Just like us, he sticks to pot and coke."

Wanda waited until Eddie had turned their silver Mercedes onto a side road behind the Bentley's pickup truck, before asking: "So, why don't we deal directly with Otis and Mindy then? Going through Ronald like this seems both unnecessary and dangerous."

But Eddie shook his head. "No, no, girl, this is the perfect setup for us. Yeah, sure, Otis is our main connection, but because he's an orangehead, he's unreliable. He can blow up or get caught, or even fucking die, without even a minute's notice. And when that happens, we don't want him saying he got the stuff directly from us. So, Ronald's our insurance policy. Because Ronald knows the risk involved, he's gonna keep an eye on Otis and warn us about any potential fuck-ups at his end."

Wanda wrinkled her forehead and made a thinking face. "Okay. What does Ronald get out of this?"

"Free weed. Which costs peanuts compared to the orange rock I'm laying on Otis."

"Okay, if you say so. But it sounds needlessly complicated to me. Particularly since you're still sending that shipment on to Milo with the circus. Or, have you changed your mind about that?"

Eddie took his eye off of the road for a second to grin over at her. "Not at all, baby. That's a sweet deal. That shipment doesn't belong to Otis, but to Cutthroat Kelly down in Elkins, and Otis knows that. And Otis knows exactly what Cutthroat Kelly will do to him if he dares mess with his shipment—the dago bastard ain't called 'cutthroat' 'cos he cut himself shaving. So, we don't need to worry 'bout that." Eddie laughed coldly. "Don't sweat it, honey. The orange'll get to Milo in one piece."

They were just pulling up now into the driveway of Gary Bentley's house, a compact two-story, with forest on either side of it.

"Dammit, Eddie," Wanda said, "your ranger friend wasn't lying that he likes the woods."

"Hey, baby," Eddie said, as he parked beside Gary's pickup truck. "This guy Gary is as straitlaced as they come. And his wife is twice as bad. So, please, no letting slip as to what we do, okay? As far as they're concerned, I'm a legit businessman, shipping fruit down south. No hint of the illegality of the business."

"No problem, baby," Wanda said as she undid her seatbelt. "I already caught on that the guy's a square when you apologized to him for swearing." She grinned at him. "Baby, I got this."

Eddie grinned back. "Yeah, that's why I love you so much."

Eddie and Wanda got out of the Mercedes and walked over to join the Bentley's.

Of course, Gary Bentley had not the slightest idea that Eddie Bush was the second man he'd noticed at the Sleepaway Campground parking lot the previous day, or that Eddie Bush was currently the largest dealer of Agent Orange in the state of West Virginia. Or, even more problematic, that Eddie and Wanda Bush currently had about ten pounds of the deadly narcotic known as Agent Orange concealed in the trunk of their Mercedes.

CHAPTER 8

Smoking weed was Ronald Reed's primary way of relaxation. Middle-aged with an estranged wife and children, Ronald didn't require any more stress than life had already dealt him. He looked after Sydney like he was paid to do, trained the kangaroo, and did his nightly performances as Bumble the Clown.

Ronald was a simple man with simple needs. No wife, no girlfriend. Just himself, his kangaroo, and as much marijuana as he could smoke.

Which was, of course, what had made him ripe for Eddie Bush's picking. Eddie had promised Ronald all the weed he could smoke, so long as he kept an eye on Otis Weibel . . . and his girlfriend Mindy.

Ronald didn't really understand why Eddie wanted to do his business through him, rather than directly with Otis himself, but he wasn't one to look a gift horse in the mouth.

Free pot is free pot. So long as I don't have to pay for my natural high, I'm good to go.

The night's Big Top show had ended at 8 p.m., an hour ago. As was normal after the show, Otis had walked off with Sydney hopping behind him, the female kangaroo being as used to him now as dog was to its owner.

Tonight, however, rather than lock Sydney inside her enclosure and then go to bed himself, Ronald had other business to attend to. He looked over at Sydney, who sat on the floor in a corner of the tent, eating an apple. The kangaroo stared back at him, wondering if he had a command for her.

Ronald did. He got up and walked over to one of his suitcases, out of which he pulled a small package. This was the Agent Orange that Eddie Bush had handed him yesterday to pass on to Otis.

Ronald studied the package, one corner of which was ripped open. That corner had snagged on the door of the circus van yesterday, when he'd been trying to get into it after negotiations with Eddie.

Ronald considered repairing the ripped corner with tape, but didn't know where he'd put the tape after its last use.

It'll do, he decided. *It just has to make a trip across the camp.*

"Here, girl," he called out to Sydney.

The kangaroo looked up from her apple and then obediently hopped over to Ronald's side. Ronald was once again surprised by how large she was. Most female kangaroos were relatively small in size, but Sydney here was almost the size of a male kangaroo. This was an advantage during the show, as it made the 'fights' seem more competitive than if she'd been a regular-sized kangaroo female.

It don't feel different when she hits me though, he thought, remembering the falls he continually had to take in his role as Bumble the clown. But the clown role was his bread and butter.

Ronald reached down Sydney's belly, pulled out the top rim of her pouch, and popped the package of Agent Orange into it.

"Okay, girl, go deliver it to Otis and Mindy like last time," Ronald said.

In response, Sydney gave him an inquiring look.

Ronald realized he'd not used the correct command the kangaroo understood.

"Otis, Otis, Otis, go," he said, and then Sydney obediently hopped off through the tent's entrance flap.

Once the kangaroo was on her way with the Agent Orange safely concealed in her pouch, Ronald fired off a text message to Otis, letting him know Sydney was on her way over. Then lay back on his bed and nodded off.

The drug would be delivered to Otis; Ronald had no doubt about that. He'd been using Sydney to courier both weed and meth to Otis for two weeks now, each time with complete success, and no one had the slightest suspicion of what was going on.

Being an animal trainer definitely had its perks.

CHAPTER 9

Sydney, the kangaroo, hopped her way over to Otis and Mindy's tent. None of the circus members paid any attention to her being outside of her enclosure.

The wire enclosure existed mainly to protect Sydney from the unwanted attentions of circus fans, some of whom might unwittingly provoke the kangaroo into defending herself, with bad results for the human, who wouldn't be expecting such a reaction from a seemingly tame animal.

Sydney had been born in captivity, and so was totally habituated to humans. Under everyday circumstances, she was no threat to anyone. Which was why she was mostly ignored as she made her way over to Otis's tent. The circus performers viewed her exactly as they would a pet dog.

By now, all of the visitors to the circus had left. And, because this was Saturday night, many of the circus personnel were themselves heading out to town to party and dance the night away. The camp was already showing signs of desertion and would soon be mostly empty.

***

Sydney arrived at Otis's camper and waited—waiting was what Ronald had trained her to do. On receiving the text Ronald had sent him, Otis would emerge and retrieve the package from Sydney's pouch. Sydney would be rewarded with a treat, either some fruit or even potato chips. The kangaroo would then hop back to Ronald's tent.

However, tonight things worked out differently. While Sydney waited patiently outside the camper door with her pouch-full of Agent Orange, Otis and Mindy had no idea that their drug shipment had arrived on their doorstep.

The two were having sex.

"Oh yeah, man, fuck me like that!" Mindy whispered in a guttural voice, while their bodies smacked together.

"Yeah, baby!" Otis grunted back. He had Mindy's ankles crossed and her legs folded over his left shoulder and was thrusting hard into her tight little hole.

They were on one of the camper's couches, with the force of their coupling rocking the camper back and forth.

Sydney sat undisturbed through the disturbance. By now she was quite used to human activities, and though she didn't completely understand what this one was about, she knew it wasn't a threat to her. And besides, the smell of sex excited her in a nice way.

So, she sat waiting.

This was however a night when disaster was scheduled to occur. Some disasters come pre-packed as such, while others need to be assembled on delivery. What was already happening here was the latter sort of disaster, the kind that needs to be pieced together.

The first element of tonight's crisis was Ronald's sending Sydney to deliver the Agent Orange. Had he made the trip himself, nothing bad would have happened.

The second element was Sydney's needing to wait for Otis and Mindy to finish fucking and attend to her.

The third element . . . that torn corner of the Agent Orange package that Ronald had neglected to repair before slipping the package into Sydney's pouch. Under normal circumstances, Ronald's oversight may not have created much of a problem. But, during the process of Sydney's hopping through the circus, the package had gotten turned upside-down . . . and about half of the Agent Orange it contained had spilled out into the kangaroo's pouch. The pouch was nice and warm, and hairless, and a bit wet, and under these optimal conditions, the surface layer of the drug quickly melted and was absorbed like a salve through Sydney's skin into her bloodstream.

And fourth . . . Well, even though animals, in general, have no real sense of the passage of time, after a while of sitting there, Sydney had become distracted by the scent of the drug she was carrying in her pouch. The smell, which intensified as the drug melted inside her pouch, soon led her to investigate it. She leaned forward, dipped her tongue into her pouch, and began licking, just like she would do if she was cleaning it out when she had a joey in there.

The Agent Orange that had entered her bloodstream through absorption was already working in her now, making her feel convulsive and jittery. And once Sydney began licking it up too, the effect only increased.

Worst yet, Sydney discovered that she liked the taste of Agent Orange. It wasn't a natural taste, but it filled the kangaroo with a sense of mad euphoria.

She found it more delicious than food.

So, Sydney the Kangaroo investigated further, dipping a paw into her pouch and scooping out the half-empty package. The drug spilled to the floor, and Sydney began eating it all up. She ate everything the package contained.

The drug worked rapidly on the kangaroo, as it generally did on animals as compared to humans.

CHAPTER 10

Inside the camper, unaware of what was happening outside, Mindy Lane finally gasped, went cross-eyed, and slumped off the couch to the floor. A moment later, Otis Weibel slumped down beside her. The pair of them lay there on the floor, breathing heavily.

"That was great," Mindy whispered to Otis, when they'd both got their breath back. "You've fucked me so good, now I just wanna fall asleep."

"Yeah, babe, you're always fantastic," Otis agreed, and then he levered himself to a sitting position beside her.

"Anything the matter?" Mindy asked.

Otis nodded and looked around for his pants with eyes that already showed faint traces of Agent Orange addiction. Mindy's eyes were similar; only she was much further gone in her drug addiction. Mindy was the one who'd introduced Otis to the killer drug, and it was merely her unusual tolerance to the drug's effects that had prevented her from having eyes that looked like ripe oranges by now.

"Yeah, there is," Otis finally replied Mindy's question. "Ronald was supposed to send Sydney over with our stuff. But . . . Okay, here it is," he finished, snatching up his pants from beneath Mindy's clothes on the camper floor. Then he fished his cell phone out of the pants pocket.

"Oh, Ronald already sent me a text."

Mindy sat up. "What's it say, baby? I could do with some orange now. It's been a while since we had any. Sometimes, the lack of it runs me close to crazy."

Otis read the text message and smiled. "According to this text, Sydney's been waiting outside the camper for fifteen minutes now." He leered at Mindy. "We were just too occupied to realize it."

"Oh goody!"

Otis got to his feet and pulled his pants on. He was a tall and thin man. Mindy was pretty and tending toward fat. Visually, they made a nice couple.

"Pass me some cookies from the fridge," Otis told Mindy when he'd gotten his pants on. "I'll send Sydney back and then we'll have ourselves a private party."

Mindy opened up the fridge and searched through it. "We're out of cookies."

"Gimme a candy bar then. The 'roo loves chocolate milk."

Mindy handed him a Snickers. Otis looked around for his sneakers, decided he didn't need them as he was just stepping outside for half a minute, and opened up the camper door.

Cool air welcomed him outside. With most of the staff headed off to town for revelry, the circus camp had the air of a deserted trailer park to it, though Otis did hear the rumbling of the lions and chittering monkeys a short distance away behind the Big Top.

The lions never understood that they'd never eat caged monkeys. The monkeys, too, didn't understand that caged lions weren't a threat to them. Both animal species continued to growl and pose like they were still somewhere in the African forests.

"Hey, Sydney, where are you?" Otis called. "Sydney, where are you?"

He stopped calling and looked around. He couldn't see the kangaroo anywhere among the deserted tents nearby.

That was strange, he thought. Sydney was a reliable drug courier; always punctual too. Ronald had trained her well; she never failed to wait until he came to her.

Otis walked around the camper until he found the kangaroo. She lay on her side with her tongue hanging out of her mouth. Her tongue was bright orange in color.

Otis winced, then knocked on the rear window of the camper until Mindy peeked through it.

"Get dressed and come outside," he mouthed at her. "We got a fucking problem."

CHAPTER 11

"Is she dead?" Mindy asked.

Otis, who was crouched over the prone kangaroo, looked up and nodded. "Dead as a doorknob."

Mindy now also bent over Sydney. "But what the heck killed her?"

Otis held up the plastic bag he'd found beside the kangaroo. "Our drug shipment did."

Mindy frowned. "Shit, man! I was really looking forward to that stuff. You know how it is when one doesn't have any orange. It feels like my guts are all tangling around themselves like mating snakes—"

"Shush!" Otis cautioned her. "Not so damn loud. Yeah, I know no one's home now, but we don't wanna draw any attention to ourselves."

"Yeah, yeah, whatever," Mindy said sulkily. "Hey, check inside her pouch and see if any of it maybe spilled inside there."

"Baby, we got bigger problems here. Like this dead kangaroo!"

"Just do it!"

So, Otis stuck his hand inside of Sydney's pouch and fished around in there. Unlike previous times when Ronald had hidden marijuana in there, the pouch was hot and sticky. Otis persevered in his search, however, and located a few pebble-like objects. He pulled these out to see what they were. They were five little orange things about the size of jellybeans, and they were horribly half-dissolved and stuck to his fingers.

"This seems to be all that's left of our orange," he told Mindy in a disgusted voice.

"It'll have to do," Mindy said. "But hey, they look disgusting. Are you sure they aren't kangaroo babies? Joeys or whatever they're called?"

Otis waved his hand at her. "Do you fucking want these or not? You're overlooking the fact that we have a dead kangaroo on our hands. A kangaroo that's one of our place-of-employment's star attractions."

Mindy picked three of the five melted orange candies off of his hand, and stuck them in her mouth.

"That's better," she said with a grin as the drug went to work on her system. "Now what the hell are we gonna do?"

Otis didn't reply to her until he'd eaten the remaining two pieces of Agent Orange and licked the gooey slick off of his fingers. A portion of his mind wanted to yell at Mindy for taking more of the drug and leaving less for him. But he managed to submerge the rage that the mere sight of the orange narcotic was triggering in him.

Then he looked at Mindy and said in a worried voice, "We're gonna have to tell Elaine."

"Oh no," Mindy said. "We can't tell her. She's gonna be furious. You already, said it, baby—Sydney is one of the show's biggest draws."

Otis stepped up next to his girlfriend and put an arm around her. "I know," he said. "But I'm even more worried about what Ronald is gonna do once he finds out. Ronald fucking loved this kangaroo."

"Elaine won't have left for town with the others," Mindy said. "She should be in her camper." The Agent Orange was working in Mindy's system now, breeding its familiar euphoria, and its even more familiar anger. Mindy was suddenly enraged at the dead kangaroo for stealing and wasting their drugs.

She pointed down at Sydney, who lay there, motionless as a rock on the floor. "But, man, she looks heavy. How do we get the thieving shithead kangaroo over to Elaine's RV?"

"I'll go find a wheelbarrow or a hand truck to put her in," Otis replied, and then he got his cell phone out of his pocket and handed it to Mindy. "While I'm gone, you call Ronald and tell him what happened. Tell him we're taking the body over to Elaine's."

Otis hurried off. Overhead, it seemed as if dark clouds had begun covering the night sky over the circus.

CHAPTER 12

When Otis returned with a wheelbarrow, they lifted Sydney onto it. Otis huffed and puffed at the effort; Sydney weighed a lot.

"Did you get Ronald?" Otis asked while they moved the dead kangaroo.

Mindy shook her head. "I called, but he didn't pick up. He must be sleeping."

"Most likely, he's stoned on pot again."

Mindy considered this. "Sounds right. But, baby, what if someone sees us moving Sydney?" She gestured around at the empty spaces between the circus tents. "Yes, almost everyone's gone off to town tonight, but a few people are still bound to be about."

"We'll cover her up," Otis said after considering her statement for a while. "Alright, come back into the RV, and let's get properly dressed."

A few minutes later, Otis and Mindy reemerged from the camper. Otis was carrying a blanket.

"I couldn't find the camper keys," Mindy said as she descended to the ground.

"Forget about locking the door. There's no one around to steal anything. Let's just get this over with."

After tucking all of the dead kangaroo's limbs properly into the confines of the wheelbarrow, Otis draped the blanket over her.

He and Mindy then set off towards Elaine's RV, which was near the animal cages behind the Big Top tent. The going was slow but uneventful. They only saw two people, two of the male acrobats, who were drunk and laughing and were headed in the opposite direction to Otis and Mindy, oblivious even to the fact that they were being observed. Then they passed a tent in which a couple was having loud sex, but saw no one.

About halfway to Elaine's camper, Otis stopped pushing the wheelbarrow and paused.

"What's the matter, baby?" Mindy asked. "You hear someone coming?"

Otis shook his head. "I suggest a change of plans," he said. "Instead of us heading for Elaine's, let's go over to Ronald's instead. We'll wake him up and tell him what happened. That way we don't have to explain to Elaine and her meathead boyfriend Cedric what the kangaroo was doing over at our camper. We'll simply lie that we went to visit Ronald, and she fell sick while we were there."

Mindy considered this. "Alright, that makes sense, too. And when we see Ronald, please fucking ask him to order us more Agent Orange from that Eddie Bush creep." Mindy gestured at the wheelbarrow with hatred in her eyes. "Man, I still can't believe this dumb fucking animal ate up all our stuff."

Otis nodded. "You're reading my mind. If she wasn't dead already, I'd kill the fucking kangaroo."

They turned back, and after a short distance, turned right and headed towards Ronald's tent.

CHAPTER 13

While Otis and Mindy were on their way over to see Ronald Reed, he in turn, and in company of Elaine Vega and her boyfriend Cedric, were on their way over to Otis and Mindy's tent.

Elaine and Cedric had been drinking, and then decided they wanted to play poker. So, they'd looked around for additional players. Since most people had either left the campground or were having sex with their partners, they'd looked for Ronald to join them, as they knew he didn't socialize much.

Ronald had agreed to play cards with them, but then, concerned as to why Sydney hadn't yet returned to his tent, he had told Elaine and Cedric that he had to pick up something from Otis and Mindy's RV on the way to theirs. Elaine and Cedric had agreed, deciding to add the couple to their poker group also.

It was on the way over there that Mindy's call (from Otis's phone) had come in, which Ronald, not wishing to discuss drugs in his employer's hearing, had naturally declined to accept.

***

"Hey, Otis . . . Mindy . . . are you home!?"

"Maybe they're having sex too!" Cedric said. "Seems like everyone is tonight 'cept us three."

"Oh, we'll be making love, too," Elaine said, giving Cedric's ass a squeeze. "After the card game, of course?"

"Hey," Ronald said. "You guys didn't say you wanted to play strip poker."

Elaine waved her bottle of wine at him. "We don't, 'cept you're interested."

Ronald shook his head, and quickly changed the subject. "Lemme see if they're in." He climbed the RV's steps and knocked on the door. The RV's interior lights were on.

"I don't think they're home. There doesn't seem to be anyone inside," he informed Elaine and Cedric.

"Try the door," Elaine said. "If it's open, we can always wait for them to come back."

"Yeah," Cedric agreed, taking the bottle from Elaine and drinking deep. "I know for sure they didn't head to town like everyone else seems to have done. We'll just wait for them to come back."

Ronald, who was by now wondering where in the world Otis, Mindy, and more importantly Sydney had gotten to, tried the door handle.

"It's open," he said.

"Great," Elaine said. "Let's all make ourselves at home." She offered the half-empty wine bottle to Ronald. "Want some?"

He shook his head and instead pulled out a joint, then searched his pockets for a lighter. When he didn't find one, he walked over into the camper kitchenette and searched there. He found a pack of matches, lit his joint, and then returned to join Elaine and Cedric in the camper's 'living room' area.

But when he returned there, both of his companions were looking in puzzlement at a large sheaf of dollar notes, held together with a rubber band, that lay on the camper's dining table.

"Where'd all that cash come from?" Ronald asked.

Cedric said, "Elaine accidentally knocked over that box, and the money spilled out of it."

"Yeah, yeah," Ronald agreed, taking a long pull from his joint. "But where the hell would Otis and Mindy find that much cash?"

"Inside Elaine's safe," Cedric replied coldly.

"What?" Ronald stared at Elaine, and she nodded back.

"Yes, someone's been stealing money from my old safe, and I think we just discovered who and who it is."

Ronald gulped and sat down. As he smoked his marijuana, he pondered what he'd just heard. There was no doubt about it; the bundle of cash did look like a day's gate takings.

Oh, so that's where Otis and Mindy got the money to buy that much Agent Orange from Eddie Bush!

But of course, Ronald couldn't tell that to Elaine and Cedric.

"What do we do now?" Cedric asked Elaine. "We know who's been stealing our money, so what now?"

"I'm not sure if I wanna hand them over to the police or just demand that they refund the rest of it," Elaine said. She slipped the recovered money into her brassiere, and then picked up her bottle of wine again. "But for now, let's just wait here till they get back."

So, the three of them sat and waited. Cedric had a deck of cards with him, so they began playing poker, using matchsticks for money.

Alright, now where the hell is Sydney? Ronald wondered as Cedric dealt the cards. *What the hell has happened to my kangaroo?*

CHAPTER 14

So far Gary's evening had been going great. After having a few beers, he and Eddie Bush had slipped back into their old camaraderie, laughing and joking as if no time at all had elapsed since they'd last seen each other.

A short while ago, they'd all had dinner and since then, Eddie had been regaling their gathering with tales from his life as a traveling salesman.

". . . And then this guy Joey, he goes running off with his hair on fire," Eddie finished his latest tale. "And we ain't seen him since."

Gary laughed. True, there was a dark thread to some of Eddie's stories, but they were all still uproariously funny.

"He went to all of that trouble to get a glass of whiskey?" Charlotte said. "That's pathetic."

"Joey was always that sort of loser," Wanda said unsympathetically. "Right now, he's in prison for doing something just as dumb."

Gary had been trying to keep track of Charlotte's drinking tonight, but, seeing as he'd had several beers himself, he must have misestimated her alcohol intake.

Charlotte saw her husband watching her, shook her head, and waved her beer at him. "Sorry, sweetheart, but I'm too drunk to accompany you back to the circus."

"Yeah, I can see that," Gary agreed. "You're drunk as a skunk on a tree stump."

Eddie looked queerly at Gary. "You're going back to the circus at . . ." he checked the time on his watch. " Half-past ten? What the hell do you want to do there?"

"He's playing private dick," Charlotte said. "And not the bedroom kind either."

Gary sighed. "Honey, please."

Charlotte giggled. "No, you, please." She nodded to Eddie and his wife. "I could do with some private dick tonight, but no, my hubby is taking it to the circus showgirls."

"You're working as a private eye?" Wanda asked. Wanda Bush had had even more to drink tonight than Charlotte, but didn't appear even slightly inebriated.

Gary explained to her and Eddie about the chunk of Agent Orange he'd found at the campground and how, during the circus performance, he'd recognized the kangaroo's trainer as one of the men he'd seen in the campground parking lot.

"That sounds serious," Eddie said, with a grave look on his face. He looked at Wanda. "What do you think, honey?"

She nodded back. "Yes, I agree. It sounds very dangerous. Why do you want to risk going back there alone, Gary? Why not tell the police what you know and let them handle it?"

" 'Cos I'm not a hundred percent certain the trainer guy had anything to do with the drug I found. Hell, I'm not even fifty or thirty percent sure. The drug could've been left there by one of the campers." He drank his beer and laughed. "You don't wanna know how many times that's happened. Anyway, what I'd planned was for Charlotte and I to slip back there tonight and just see if we found anything suspicious."

"Sorry, but I can't go with you," Charlotte said. "Don't be mad, honey."

Gary smiled at her. "I ain't mad at you. I'll just call off the plan."

"We'll go with ya," Eddie volunteered.

Gary looked at him in surprise. "Why? I ain't even sure there's anything to find there."

"Eddie can't stand drug dealers," Wanda said. "A group of them tried to hurt me some years ago. Eddie had to shoot one of them."

Gary looked from Wanda to Eddie. "That true, man?"

Eddie looked embarrassed. "Well, I only shot the guy in the foot, ya know. But yeah, Wanda's right. I can't stand people who make money off of the misery of others." He frowned. "So, if you're on any kind of an antidrug crusade, sign me up."

Gary smiled. "Okay, let's go then." He looked at Wanda, and gestured at Charlotte. "Can you stay here with her till we get back? We shouldn't take more than an hour to just look around."

Wanda shook her head. "Uh-uh. Where Eddie goes, I go. And this sounds very exciting. I'm coming with you men."

Gary wanted to protest that she'd slow them down, but Eddie shook his head at him. "Don't waste your breath. No one can change her mind once it's made up."

Gary missed the sly, amused look that passed between husband and wife after Eddie said this. Charlotte didn't miss the look, but she was too drunk to attach any meaning to it.

"Okay, let's go," Gary said. He frowned at Charlotte. "Please, hon, no more drinking tonight."

"Why?" Charlotte asked. "I'm not driving anywhere, am I?"

CHAPTER 15

Of course, Eddie's claim to hate drug dealers was total bullshit.

The real reason why Eddie and Wanda Bush were following Gary back to the circus tonight was because of the package of Agent Orange they had in the trunk of the Mercedes. The drug was supposed to be delivered to Otis and his girlfriend Mindy to, in turn, be delivered by them to Cutthroat Kelly over in Elkin's, where Madam Vega's Travelling Show was due to visit next weekend.

This was the original reason why Eddie and Wanda had visited the circus in the afternoon, but after the first show ended, Ronald had been nowhere in sight. And then they'd run into the Bentleys anyway.

***

Eddie Bush wanted to ship that load of Agent Orange to Cutthroat Kelly in Elkin's so they could break the local monopoly on the drug. It was frustrating to both dealers how Agent Orange— probably the most addictive narcotic ever created, came into the market in fits and starts. Like feast or famine. One week, you had an excess of it, and the addicts were overjoyed, and the next week, you'd wondered if the drug actually existed; it would become that scarce to find.

And from what Eddie had heard, there was a fierce rivalry between the local chemists to corner the Agent Orange market.

Max Carillo, the original guy who'd created the orange-crack hybrid had gotten whacked, then Doyle Sanders, the guy who'd taken over production from him had gotten whacked too. In both cases, the stories as to how the men had died made little sense.

The Agent Orange which Eddie was dealing now came from a secret source. Most likely from fear of being whacked too, the new chemist guy didn't want anyone knowing who he was. He did have a reliable supply line, but both Eddie and Cutthroat knew it was simply a matter of time till he shared the same unfortunate fate as his predecessors.

So, they wanted to start manufacturing for themselves. It was the smartest thing to do.

Cutthroat now had a new chemist working for him, one of his nerdy nephews, and the kid believed he could analyze Agent Orange and determine how to synthesize it from ordinary cocaine.

Cutthroat said the kid was a genius—had graduated cum laude in chemistry from Harvard University—so maybe this was the break they'd been looking for. All they needed was a sufficiently large amount of Agent Orange for the kid to work with.

If Cutthroat's nephew really could do this, it meant big bucks for both Eddie and Cutthroat Kelly, and big problems for both US law enforcement and the law-abiding American taxpayer.

***

"This works out well for us, don't'cha think?" Eddie asked Wanda as they drove behind Gary. Their excuse for not riding with him in his ranger truck was that they wanted to be able to drive straight home after their joint excursion.

Wanda laughed. "This is a fucking comedy. So, he actually saw you and Ronald at the campground?"

Eddie laughed. "The poor sucker didn't know you were in the car too."

The two vehicles rolled over the night-darkened roads in a direct reversal of the route that had brought them to the Bentley's countryside residence.

"What do we do when we arrive there?" Wanda asked as Eddie slowed down to follow the pickup truck ahead of them around a corner. "We can't deliver the shit to Ronald if Ranger Danger is tagging along."

"Don't sweat it. Once we arrive there, I'll go talk to Gary and hurry him on ahead while you get the stuff out of the car trunk and put it in your purse. Then you can hurry after us and catch up. Then, later on, we'll find a way to ditch the guy for a while."

"That's easy to do—we'll just do like they do in the movies: split up and search separately, then meet up ahead."

"Good girl," Eddie said, reaching across the front of the Mercedes and patting her on the shoulder. "You never, ever, lose the fucking plot."

CHAPTER 16

Otis and Mindy pushed the wheelbarrow through the entrance flap of Ronald's tent.

"He ain't here," Mindy said. "We walked all that way and he ain't here."

"He probably just stepped outside to pee," Otis said, parking the wheelbarrow in the middle of the tent.

Mindy gestured down at the covered-up kangaroo. "Hey, do you think he maybe went over to our place to look for Sydney?"

"Maybe," Otis agreed. "If he did, we'd have missed him because we didn't come here directly, but were originally headed for Elaine's place."

"So, what do we do now? Wait, or call him?"

Otis gestured down at Ronald's mattress. "Let's wait a bit. If he ain't back in five, then we'll call him."

After they'd both settled down on the thick mattress, Mindy said, "Baby, what're we gonna do about drugs? That taste of Agent Orange we just had was far from enough." She looked over at the wheelbarrow with sufficient venom in her gaze to freeze the dead kangaroo to stone, if such were possible. "I can't believe that that shithead animal ate . . . dammit!"

"Calm down, baby. Ronald already told us Eddie's bringing the shipment we're taking to Elkin's over tonight. We can always help ourselves to some of that."

Mindy's eyes widened in fright. "You can't seriously be thinking of ripping off Cutthroat Kelly. The guy will gut us both like fish if we use his drugs."

Otis shook his head. "No, he won't, 'cos he won't know we took it. We don't need to deliver the goods to Cutthroat until next weekend when the circus arrives in Elkin's. So we'll use part of it tonight and replace it with the stuff we're gonna have Ronald order from Eddie Bush for us tonight."

Mindy thought on that. "Yeah, we can afford to pay for it. We do still have that cash we stole from Elaine's safe." Then she looked worried again. "Baby, I really got a bad feeling about us ripping off Elaine like this. It can't go on much longer. Soon, we'll be caught, maybe even the next time you sneak in there."

That was their stealing arrangement. Mindy acted as the lookout, while Otis entered Elaine's camper and stole the money. They could open Elaine's safe because Otis had once been in Elaine's camper when circus accountant Kevin Lagen was putting money into it and he had managed to memorize the combination for the lock. Once away from Elaine's camper, Otis had written down the combination and stored it for future reference.

That had happened three months ago, long ago enough that even Kevin would never connect this week's missing money to the day that Elaine Vega had sent Otis to fetch her laptop from her camper.

"Listen," Otis told Mindy. "I don't intend to steal anything more from Elaine . . . not for a long while. By now, she, Cedric, and Kevin must be keeping an eye out for—hey, what the hell was that?"

Mindy had been examining her blue and white manicure, which was styled to match her blue and white stage costume. "What was what?"

"I just heard a noise," Otis said.

Mindy didn't look up from studying her nails. "Most likely, it's Ronald returning from the crapper."

"I don't think so, Mindy. It sounded like it came from inside here."

"It was just a rat then."

Otis tapped Mindy on the leg. "Look!"

Mindy looked, because now she could hear the sound, too. And its source was also obvious. The wheelbarrow was shaking, vibrating so much that it was shifting over the ground.

"What the heck?" Mindy said. "So, the kangaroo wasn't dead?"

"That's a relief," Otis said, getting to his feet. He smiled. "Now we don't have to worry about what Ronald or Elaine are gonna say."

Mindy stood up also. "Yeah, but if Sydney is still alive, why is the wheelbarrow shaking like she's got a fever?"

"Only one sure way to find out." Otis pulled the blanket off of the wheelbarrow.

Yes, Sydney was shaking like crazy in there. After Otis removed the blanket that had been covering her, the kangaroo's shaking became so pronounced that the wheelbarrow was almost leaping from side to side.

Mindy had now stepped up beside the wheelbarrow. "It looks like we're going to need a vet," she said.

"Right. Soon as Ronald gets back."

"Otis, maybe we should call him already. This looks serious. Sydney could die; for real this time."

So, Otis got out his phone. But then, all of a sudden, the wheelbarrow fell over, and the kangaroo spilled out onto the tent's floor.

"Shit, she ain't dead, is she?" Mindy asked. "That's really gonna suck."

"No, she's not dead," Otis said, as the prone kangaroo now slowly got back up to her feet.

"Well, that's the effect of too much Agent Orange for you," Mindy said. "Now, Sydney's got giant orange eyes. How the fuck are we gonna explain that to the circus's customers?"

"We'll best leave that for Elaine to figure . . . hey, hey, Sydney, calm down," Otis added as the kangaroo took up her classic boxing stance and began hopping about with her head striking the low roof of the tent each time."

Mindy nodded. "Yeah, Sydney, calm down. We're not putting on a show now." She looked around Ronald's tent for something to feed the kangaroo, who seemed to be caught in a weird tension. "Where the hell does Ron keep the kangaroo's food?"

"I think her food's in the cooler over there. No, wait, I've still got that candy bar in my—"

But before Otis finished speaking, Sydney punched him, striking him in the chest.

Otis felt pain then like he'd never felt before, and when he looked down he understood why. The kangaroo's forepaw was stuck deep inside the left side of his chest.

Actually, Otis, who was already dying by then, never realized the full extent of the bodily trauma that the kangaroo's punch had caused him.

Mindy, who was standing behind Otis at that point, saw Sydney's paw emerge through Otis's back, with his heart speared on her claws.

Otis remained upright, dead on his feet, until Sydney jerked her paw out of his body. Then, while Otis collapsed to the floor, with blood flowing out of the gaping hole in his chest, the killer kangaroo clasped his heart in her front paws and took a bite out of it.

Mindy shrieked, but the sound was a strangled one. She suddenly understood that the drug Agent Orange had totally messed up this kangaroo. The animal wasn't much larger, but she was much more muscular, with longer claws on both fore- and hind-paws; and of course, she now had those horrible bulging eyes, eyes like glowing streetlamps, or rotting oranges.

After eating some more bites of Otis's heart, the kangaroo dropped the organ on its dead owner and looked over in Mindy's direction. Blood dripped from Sydney's mouth. The kangaroo also hissed at Mindy, revealing longer teeth than she'd previously had.

Mindy turned and fled, with the kangaroo bounding after her.

CHAPTER 17

Outside of the tent, Mindy ran for her dear life. She ran without care for direction.

She wanted to scream for help, and almost did so. But then Sydney leapt over the tent she was running past and landed in front of her.

Mindy both froze in position and clammed her lips up tight.

Sydney had landed ahead of her, and hadn't turned around, meaning the kangaroo hadn't noticed her. Mindy definitely didn't want Sydney to notice her. In her mind's eye, she could clearly see the kangaroo's bloody forepaw emerging through the splintered bones of Otis's back, with his still-beating heart squirting blood over it.

That won't be happening to me, she decided. *So, I'd better keep quiet. The kangaroo hasn't noticed me yet. Shit! Where do I go now? Who the hell will still be around?* She felt her pockets for her cell phone. *No, I left it in the camper. Otis's cell phone is back in Ronald's tent with his body.*

Sydney was meanwhile hopping on the spot and shadowboxing. Mindy made herself as inconspicuous as she could against the tent and continued her panicky thinking:

Betty and Mary were having sex when Otis and I walked past their tent. I can use their cell phone to call the cops. I'd better run over there. No, our own RV is much closer, I'd better go over there.

Mindy stepped out of concealment and hurried across a gap between two tents into concealment again. Behind her, she heard Sydney snorting, hissing, and, of course, hopping around.

Good, just fifty or so yards more to go, Mindy thought. She hurried forward past a trailer and then froze again, when Sydney once more came hopping down out of the air and landed in front of her.

How the hell is she able to leap so high now? Mindy wondered in fright. *And how could she punch through Otis's body like that? Even a muscular human being can't do that! It's like the Agent Orange has endowed Sydney with superpowers!*

Not to be outdone by the kangaroo, Mindy chose another route between the circus tents. Of course, she was very frightened, but she was too close to her cell phone now to not make the attempt to reach it.

However, once she'd made a little progress, the kangaroo came down again, landing with a mighty thump barely five yards in front of Mindy.

Mindy almost howled in frustration when she saw that Sydney was once more blocking off the route to her and Otis's camper.

Mindy now suspected that the kangaroo was doing so intentionally.

It's like she's toying with me like a cat does to a mouse before it kills it! She knows where I am, but wants me to suffer. Damn sadistic crackhead animal.

Mindy felt like screaming loudly now, but she knew that if she opened her mouth and did so, she'd be as good as dead.

She began thinking hard, wondering what she could do to survive being killed by this insane orange-eyed crack-addict kangaroo.

CHAPTER 18

It is, of course, hardly conceivable to the rational mind that a kangaroo should be able to force its paw all the way through a man's ribs, rip out his heart, and then punch its way out through his shoulder blade in a single motion. Even a bullet would have difficulty making that journey (minus detaching the heart, of course) without stopping somewhere along the way.

It is also inconceivable that a regular kangaroo should be capable of making twenty-foot leaps up into the air, bounds that carry it all the way over tents and trailers.

Welcome to the wacky, impossible world of the Agent-Orange-addicted animal.

No proper explanations of their transformations had been given because no proper research had so far been carried out on 'orangehead' animals. What was known about their extraordinary capacities for violence and feats of strength had been observed while they'd been killing their victims. And afterward, most of these observations had been ridiculed by the scientific community.

But there it was. Possibly because it was never designed for them, Agent Orange worked strange and crazy magic on the bodies of its animal (and cryptid and insect) users. In addition to always giving them glowing oversized eyes, it generally increased their muscle bulk and also ramped up their muscle tension, which meant they were always much stronger than they looked.

Mentally, such animals lost any previous timidity in their nature, and specifically their fear of mankind.

In fact, even those crackhead animals that had previously been vegetarian began to look on humans as food.

In more ways than one, an Agent-Orange-addicted animal was a very dangerous and deadly creature to have to deal with.

And poor little Sydney the Kangaroo, the much-loved boxing attraction of Madam Vega's Travelling Show, had now become one such animal.

CHAPTER 19

Sydney's warped mind was a swirl of emotions, most of them violent.

Mindy had been correct in her assessment of her situation. Sydney *was* playing with her. As the kangaroo hopped around, she at all times kept part of her mind on the terrified human being nearby, thrilling in the knowledge that the woman was completely at her mercy, and she could kill and eat her anytime she wanted.

Yes, she would kill and eat Mindy, but not yet.

The narcotic in Sydney's system was making her restless. Her senses felt amplified; she could smell people near and far off. They smelled delicious to her, so much so that her brain almost overloaded on the sheer anticipation of what they'd taste like when she had them in her clutches and was biting bits out of them.

Humans were like large walking-and-talking apples that bled.

Sydney was finally tired of her hopping game. Her restlessness finally demanded action from her. She could smell the woman directly behind her, and so she turned and looked that way. The woman was hiding behind a pushcart.

Sydney hopped forward a little, and sniffed the air. She hopped forward a little more, and the woman dashed out of cover and ran for her life.

Sydney watched her go, and she let her feel she had an actual chance of making it to safety, and then, just before the woman would have run through the entrance of the giant Big Top tent, Sydney leapt through the air, covering twenty yards with a single bound, and landed in front of the woman.

Sydney turned around. The woman screamed and ran off in the opposite direction. Now enjoying the chase, the kangaroo prepared to leap after her. But then, she sniffed the air and froze where she stood.

What was that tantalizing smell? The odor was distant, but approaching fast. It commanded her full attention. Then she understood what it was. Humans in cars were bringing more Agent Orange this way.

Of course, the rampaging kangaroo had no idea that the orange stuff was called Agent Orange. But she knew that she had loved the strange orange nuts the first time she'd eaten them, and now her mind and body were suddenly exploding with desire for a repeat taste.

So, the crack-addicted kangaroo let Mindy get away from her. What she could smell approaching her now was of a much higher priority.

But from long association with them, Sydney knew that humans were themselves dangerous. Except when unavoidable, it was best to hunt them singly, not when they were in groups. Mindy alone was easy prey. Two Mindys would have been complicated. And there were three humans in the approaching vehicles.

Biding her time to strike, Sydney the kangaroo leapt back into the wide range of shadows thrown by the Big Top and waited.

CHAPTER 20

"So, we're here," Eddie Bush said as the silver Mercedes rolled into the temporary circus ground.

On their first visit, neither Eddie nor Wanda had really paid any attention to the circus camp's layout. There had been too many other attendees; everywhere one looked, one faced a sea of people. But tonight, with the grounds deserted and just a quarter-moon in the sky, husband and wife had a clearer impression of where they'd arrived.

"This place looks creepy," Wanda said as they rolled beneath the 'WELCOME TO MADAM VEGA'S TRAVELING SHOW!' banner over the gates. This far out in the countryside, the circus only had a front wall that was wooden, gaudily painted, and reusable.

Gary had already parked his Ranger truck inside the circus grounds, a short distance behind the welcome sign. Eddie followed suit but left a few yards of space between the vehicles. He could easily explain the separation by the need to not get in one another's way in the event of their needing to make a fast escape.

"Okay, baby, remember the plan," Eddie told Wanda after turning off the engine. "I'll go distract Mr. Boy Scout over there while you retrieve our stuff. If he asks you anything 'bout what you were doing in the trunk, just say you were looking for the other pair of shoes you sometimes leave in there. Got it?"

Wanda nodded. "Got it." She tapped the glove compartment with her fingernails. "Are we packing heat?"

Eddie shook his head. "Regretfully, no, we don't take any guns with us."

"Eddie, this could be dangerous."

"Not really, baby, 'cos the drug dealers our naïve ranger friend Gary is here to look for are actually you and me, who came here with him. And we don't plan on shooting him, do we? Not after we all just got through sharing such a pleasant evening."

Wanda giggled. "Listen to you. You're drunk."

Eddie laughed. "Maybe. Hey, we're all drunk. But the main reason why we don't carry any guns into the fairground tonight—and that includes that little .22 firecracker of yours—is 'cos I'm supposed to be an everyday businessman, not some badass."

"I don't like it, Eddie. This place looks creepy in the dark like this. What if something goes wrong, and we need our heat?"

"Hon, you don't gotta like it. Just do it, like the Nike ad says."

Eddie turned off the car light and got out.

"Hey, babe, remember you don't make a move till I'm over there with Gary."

"Yeah, yeah, man."

CHAPTER 21

While Eddie Bush was making arrangements with Wanda in their car, Gary was already out of his ranger truck. He locked it up, walked to the rear of the vehicle, and waited. Except for a few RVs parked near the Big Top, this makeshift parking lot area was empty of cars. Gary kicked a clod of sod as he smelt the fresh night air. He wondered if Charlotte had gone to bed now or if she was still drinking.

Yeah, I guess that's why the law always advises not to drink and drive, he thought, on realizing he was himself a little unsteady on his feet. *In fact, what the hell am I thinking? Or wasn't thinking, maybe? If the cops had stopped us on our drive up here, either Eddie or I would've failed a breathalyzer test; that's for certain. We've all been drinking for hours.*

Gary looked over at Eddie, who was just getting out of the Mercedes, while Wanda remained seated inside it. The first time he'd glanced over at them, the couple had been laughing. Now, Wanda had a sour look on her face.

I don't know why it is, but I don't trust that woman. She's got gold-digger written all over her. Eddie's a stand-up sorta guy, but that wife of his? Nah, I just don't feel right about her. And yet, Charlotte's taken to her like fish take to water.

Eddie was saying something to Wanda through the window, and Gary began feeling impatient.

Those two are acting like we're on some kinda sightseeing trip here. Like we're here to get the animals' autographs after the show.

Now tapping his foot in his impatience to commence their investigation, Gary looked away from the Mercedes and over at the campground. Suddenly, he gaped in confusion.

What the hell is that?

Gary blinked and looked again, but it was gone. Now he tried to make sense of what he'd seen, tried to convince himself that he'd actually seen it:

I'm not crazy, am I? I just thought I saw a kangaroo leaping over a tent, heading towards us.

Gary wiped his eyes with his fingers and looked again. But there was no repeat. Whatever he'd observed was gone.

He felt shaken, however, and almost jumped in fright when Eddie clamped a hand on his shoulder.

"Hey, bro, let's get a move on," Eddie said.

Gary just refrained himself from making the customary, "Man, you scared the shit out of me" comment. It wouldn't do for a tough park ranger like himself to appear to be jumpy.

He nodded at Eddie. "Finally, man. You guys sure were taking your time in there."

Eddie laughed. "Ah, man, you know women. Earlier, she didn't want to stay back at your place, and was acting all tough and determined to come along. And now that we're here, you know what the broad says?" Eddie shook his head in confusion. "She said her feet hurt, and she wanted to rest them for a while."

Gary nodded. "Maybe she should wait for us in the car."

"No need to," Eddie said quickly. She should have a spare pair of shoes in the trunk of the car. I just hope they're flat-soles, or she's going to be griping all night." Eddie gestured towards the circus. "So, what are we doing now?"

"Do we wait for Wanda?" Gary said.

Eddie shook his head. "No. We've no idea how long she'll be. Let's just head over there ourselves. Once Wanda sees us leaving her behind, she'll shake a leg."

"Alright, then," Gary agreed.

"Are you carrying a gun on you?" Eddie asked.

Gary nodded, and tapped his waist. "Yeah, I got my service pistol on me."

"Are you sure that's wise? We're the intruders here. We can get into a lot of trouble with the cops. We could even be charged with attempted armed robbery."

"I'll take my chances. I'm not expecting to shoot anyone, but I don't want anyone shooting at us, either. You're a businessman, Eddie. You've no idea how ruthless drug dealers can be. It'll be nothing to them to bury all three of us in some dark hole out here and afterwards dump our cars elsewhere."

Eddie smiled and nodded. "I guess you're right on that point. I'll trust your professional judgment, *ranger*. Come on, let's go."

So, they set off toward the circus tents, where, except for a few desultory lights, and what might've been animal noises, all was dark and silent.

"Now remember, we need to be quiet," Gary told Eddie. "We don't wanna accidentally wake anyone up. That would automatically make us trespassers."

"I get that," Eddie agreed as they crunched along over the grass and sand. "But what exactly are we looking for here? Back at your house, it seemed to make sense to me that we're coming to search here. But now, maybe the beers are wearing off or something, 'cos now that I'm looking at how large this area is, it seems like a wild goose chase."

Gary repressed a sigh. Eddie had taken the words right out of his mouth. Now that they were about to get down to searching, what exactly *were* they searching for?

Hearing a noise behind them, Gary glanced back at their parked vehicles. Wanda had just opened the trunk of the Mercedes. Gary turned his attention back to the woman's husband.

"Just keep a look out for anything unusual, something odd that might indicate drugs or drug dealers or drug users."

"That sounds like finding a needle in a haystack."

Gary nodded. "I know it does. Oh, speaking of unusual, Eddie . . . right before we walked away from the parking lot—before you joined me by my truck—did you notice anything odd?"

Eddie frowned at Gary. "I dunno what you mean. Odd, how?"

Gary shrugged. "Like an animal acting strange or something? A kangaroo leaping ridiculously high?"

"Alright, man, now you're starting to creep me out." Eddie gestured around them. "There's no animals around here. It's the dead of night, and I think they're all in their cages asleep."

Gary didn't comment. He'd clearly imagined seeing a kangaroo leaping over a tent.

But somehow, even that realization didn't relieve him much.

CHAPTER 22

In Otis and Mindy's trailer, the poker match between Ronald, Elaine Vega, and Cedric was still on. Elaine's bottle of wine was long finished, but the alcohol had since been replaced with a bottle of whiskey from the camper fridge, with Elaine reasonably explaining to her two employees that this wasn't theft, as the money used to purchase the booze had very likely been stolen from her.

"I wonder where those two thieves got off to," Cedric said. "It ain't like we can wait up all night for them to get back here."

Ronald yawned. "Yeah, I was already sleepy when you called for me to join you for your card game. Now, I'm so sleepy, I'm not sure how I'll make it back to my tent."

Elaine, who had been winning at their poker game for a while now, laughed. "You two just don't want me to clean you out."

"You've already cleaned me out," Ronald said, after sipping from his whiskey glass. He pointed to the pile of matchsticks in front of Elaine, while both he and Cedric had none. "If you weren't my boss, I'd accuse you of cheating."

Cedric nodded. "If you weren't both my boss and my girlfriend, I'd also accuse you of cheating."

Elaine laid down her cards. "Alright, I'll admit it, I am fucking cheating. But both of you are such useless card players; you deserved to be taken to the cleaners." With a grand gesture, she brushed her pile of won matches off the table. "I just wish we'd been playing for actual money instead of—"

The camper door burst open then, and Mindy rushed inside.

"Oh, here she is!" Elaine Vega said, leaping to her feet. "Grab her, Cedric!"

Cedric obliged instantly, grabbed hold of Mindy and held her in a viselike grip. It wasn't lost on any of the three of them that Mindy didn't seem concerned that she was being so restrained.

"Help! Help," she moaned. "Sydney's killed Otis!"

"What?" Ronald, Elaine, and Cedric yelled as one.

"Did you just say Sydney killed Otis?" Ronald asked. "That's impossible! Sydney would never do a thing like that!"

Mindy didn't reply. She burst into tears and wept and wept.

"Ha, lying bitch!" Elaine said, stepping inside the camper kitchenette and picking up a long knife. When she reemerged she held the knife to Mindy's throat. "You're just saying that 'cos you know we know you stole my money!"

"I'm not! It's true!" Mindy protested.

"It can't be true!" Ronald also protested.

"I'll show you what's true," Elaine Vega said, nicking Mindy's throat so she bled a little. "Now, confess, you stupid bitch. Have you and Otis been stealing my money or not?"

"Better tell the truth, or I'll break both of your arms," Cedric warned Mindy. "You won't be able to use either of them for months." He already had her arms pinned behind her and now he tightened his grip, making her orange-tinted eyes bug out with pain.

"Yes, we'll tell the cops that you fell out of the camper while you were drunk," Elaine said, nicking Mindy's neck again. Though not exactly drunk, Elaine had too much alcohol in her system to care about the rightness or wrongness of what she herself was doing.

"Alright, alright, it's true," Mindy admitted. "Otis and I have been stealing circus money from your safe."

"That's exactly what I wanted to know." Elaine then nodded to Cedric. "Release her."

Cedric released Mindy, who slumped down onto the couch. Elaine put down her knife beside the cards on the table.

"Now, Mindy, where the hell *is* Otis?" she asked. "Talk, before I feed you to the lions."

Mindy stared up at the other three in the camper through tears. "That's what I'm trying to tell you all. Otis is fucking dead. Roland's fucking boxing kangaroo punched his heart out and then ate it. And then it began chasing me, too, to kill me and eat me, too."

"What!?" her three listeners once again repeated.

"Mindy, are you sure of this?" Roland asked.

Mindy nodded and wiped her eyes. "Yeah, yeah. Sydney ate up all of the orange you sent us, and then we thought she'd died, so we carried her to your tent . . . and once there she . . . she . . ."

"She's lying," Elaine said. "She and Otis are planning to run away."

"How 'bout if we go check out her story?" Ronald suggested.

Cedric nodded and said to Elaine, "Yeah, something's sure as hell gotten Mindy as scared as this, and it can't be the fear of you discovering she and Otis had been stealing from you. She was frightened out of her wits when she ran in here. And that was before she knew we'd discovered the theft."

Elaine nodded. "Very well then. Let's all go over to Ronald's tent and see for ourselves. Then, if Sydney has actually killed Otis, we can call the cops. We can already be sure, though, that she's hallucinating about Sydney eating Otis's heart."

"But I'm not hallucinating!"

Elaine frowned at Mindy. "Girl, you're a drug addict—a hardcore junkie. Don't look so surprised that I know. I make it my business to know everything essential about my staff; it's how I keep the business going and turning a profit." She sighed. "I keep both you and Otis on because you're good workers . . . but now . . ."

She gestured to the others. "Okay, let's go to Ronald's tent and see for ourselves."

"Oh no, I'm not going back there!" Mindy yelped. "I don't wanna see that again!"

"You don't have a fucking choice in the matter," Cedric told Mindy, then dragged her up to her feet. "Just do what the boss says.

You're in enough trouble already for stealing circus money. Don't add stupidity to your offenses."

"Just be grateful we're not going to report you to the police," Elaine said. "You and Otis will pay the stolen money back in installments." She frowned. "But, Mindy, any more crap out of you tonight, and I may change my mind and call the cops to jail you both instead."

This threat seemed to knock the wind out of Mindy. "I'm not lying. I'm not . . ." she did begin protesting again. But then the warning look that came into Elaine's angry eyes made her shut up.

Elaine nodded at Cedric. "Keep an eye on her, dear." Then she gestured to Ronald with her chin. "Let's all go."

They left the camper then; Cedric and Mindy in the lead, Elaine Vega in the middle, and Ronald last.

As a last-minute mental precaution before leaving the RV, Ronald picked up the knife Elaine had dropped and stuck it in his belt. Then he hurried down after the others.

CHAPTER 23

Sydney could smell that the little orange nuts she wanted were very close now. But the humans who had it were still sticking together. She began hopping about in frustration, but only little hops, of course, because she didn't want the humans to realize that she was very close to them. But as her frustration built up, Sydney began hopping in random directions, until, without understanding what she'd done, hopped around to the rear of the circus where the animal cages were all kept.

She had been around here before. Unlike herself, who had the run of the camp, the other animals were all caged. Her orange eyes beaming like lamps, she hopped over to the cages for a closer look. Most of the monkeys were fast asleep, but the two that noticed the transformed kangaroo both ran whimpering for the far side of the trailer cage and hid behind the branches and leaves piled there.

Sydney hopped closer and decided to bite one of the slumbering monkeys. The monkey was sleeping right next to the cage bars, and Sydney's jaws could easily fit between them.

The slumbering animal's flesh smelt delicious to her, almost as nice as humans did. She couldn't wait to taste the monkey's blood.

But before she could carry out her plan, Sydney the Kangaroo was distracted by a noise. Nearby, a lion was urinating. The reek of its urine was so pungent and inviting that Sydney lost all of her interest in eating the sleeping monkey's leg.

Sydney hopped over to look at the lion.

This particular lion was called Caesar. Of course, Sydney didn't know this, but she did know that she disliked this particular lion. Two other lions were asleep in the extensive cage, but after urinating Caesar walked across to the cage's bars and stared at Sydney.

Yes, Sydney disliked this lion, and all the lions in the circus. They smelt of 'predator' to her and 'predator' implied danger and fear, emotions that were unpleasant. But now, she couldn't actually remember what fear was—it was something divorced from her new nature. Now, she understood caution, but fear was something from a past life.

Caesar however, could not know this. Where he was concerned, he was still king of the jungle, even if, in this case, his kingdom was only sixty square feet in size and surrounded by iron bars.

For his part, Caesar instinctively knew kangaroos were good to eat. He felt frustrated that there was a large herbivore so close to him, and yet, because of the iron bars separating them, she, the kangaroo, could have been a million miles distant.

He began growling at her in a low rumble.

Sydney understood that the lion wanted to eat her. His growling recreated 'fear' in her.

Fear. Fear. Fear.

Sydney hated the returning fear, so she hopped close to the bar and punched the lion, her forepaw slipping easily between two of the cage bars and connecting with the lion's head.

The lion staggered back at the impact of the punch, but then rammed himself at the cage walls in anger. He tried to force his head between the bars and kill the disrespectful and annoying kangaroo, but this was of course impossible.

Sydney punched the lion two more times in quickly succession.

Whap! Whap!

Caesar the lion collapsed to the floor, with the front of his head completely caved in, his lower jaw completely dislocated, and the shattered bones of his face driven directly into his brain, killing him. A pool of blood slowly spread out from Caesar's head and dripped through the front of the cage.

Sydney drank her fill of the blood. True, lion blood didn't taste as sweet as human blood, but it was still pretty good.

After she drank her fill of lion's blood, Sydney cocked a leg high and urinated into the lion cage, letting rip a long hot stream of piss to let the two sleeping lions understand exactly who had killed the king of the jungle. Then she turned and hopped away.

The kangaroo felt satisfied that she would have no future trouble from the circus lions.

CHAPTER 24

"Why'd you men desert me back there?" Wanda asked when she caught up with Gary and Eddie amidst the tents.

"You were slowing us down, baby," Eddie said disinterestedly. "We couldn't wait all night for you to join us. Well, did you get your change of footwear?" He glanced down and shook his head. "I see you didn't. And why, baby, why are you bringing your handbag along now of all times?"

"I-I-I didn't wanna leave it behind in the car, in case someone breaks the glass."

"Wanda, Gucci designer or not, it's still just a fucking piece of stitched leather. Ain't no one gonna steal your damn handbag—"

"Keep it down, you two," Gary grumbled, with a backward glance at the pair. He, too, agreed that it was silly of Wanda to bring her handbag here, but what was done was done. This wasn't the place to argue about that.

Once again, had Gary Bentley been less preoccupied with his current quest, he'd have noticed Eddie's satisfied smirk after he'd cautioned them. What he wouldn't have noticed, however, was the covert thumbs-up Eddie gave Wanda when he'd looked away from them again and was once more giving the circus camp his full attention.

With no visitors here except the three of them, and night shadows everywhere, the circus lay spread out like a donut. To a degree, the arrangement of tents was a logical one, with the Big Top tent in the middle and the other tents, the trailers, and the circus staff's RVs spread around it in two concentric circles, neither of which was complete. The outer circle had opening at its sides to permit visitor transit and the inner circle was open in the front to grant access to the Big Top and all the stands and stalls.

And then there were a few tents that didn't really fit into the concentric logic, like the one behind which Gary Bentley and the Bushes were concealed.

"So, where are we starting to search from?" Wanda said.

"We've already begun," Gary replied. "Just keep your eyes open, and let me know if you see or hear anything odd."

"Admirable as your plan is," Wanda said with a yawn, "it might've been better if we'd come here on a night when there were people around. This place looks deserted."

"Yeah, it does," Gary agreed. "Better for us, though."

"My point being," Wanda said, "that we're here looking for drug-related activity. Such activity always involves people. If there's no people, no-one will be doing drugs."

"Keep your damn voice down," Eddie told her. "You'll alert people to our presence."

"Eddie, you're not listening to me. That's my whole point—that there *aren't* any people here." She fell silent as she heard the sound of an arriving vehicle. "Except maybe those guys, who're just returning home."

Gary was tired of the couple's arguments. He already realized it would have been simpler to have come alone. But in the event that he did actually stumble on something, he'd wanted at least one corroborating witness.

And now he had something else to deal with.

"Hey, guys," he told Eddie and Wanda after turning to face them. "I need to take a piss. The beers, you know."

Eddie nodded. "Okay, we'll wait here."

Gary hurried off, looking for where he could empty his bladder.

***

Eddie waited till Gary was out of sight, then nodded at Wanda.

"Okay, baby, let's get the hell out of here."

"You ain't gonna wait like you promised?"

Eddie shook his head. "Use your smarts. This is the perfect opportunity. Ronald's tent is a hundred yards away from here. With any luck, we'll be back here before Gary is. And if we ain't, we'll tell him we heard someone coming and had to hide." He gestured at Wanda's bulging handbag. "It's all in there? Everything?"

She nodded. "Yeah, but I had to throw out all my cosmetics and stuff to fit it in."

"Screw your damn cosmetics. If this deal with Cutthroat works out as planned, I'll buy you a whole fucking beauty salon."

Wanda smiled. "Okay, baby. But I'm gonna hold you to your word."

They set off at a fast walk, hurrying to be out of sight in case Gary came back early.

***

Right after they'd disappeared around the side of a tent, Gary Bentley arrived back from relieving himself. He'd located a chemical toilet that was thankfully unlocked.

"Hey, guys," he whispered. "Eddie . . . Wanda . . . where are you?"

It took him about a minute of peering cautiously about and calling out to his two friends to realize that they weren't around there anymore.

On that realization, Gary sighed in relief. *For the moment, at least, I don't care where they are, so long as they don't alert the circus folks to our presence here with their dumb squabbling.*

He looked left and right, north and south. *Alright, now, which direction do I search first?* What Wanda had said came back to his mind: *If there are no people, no one will be doing drugs.*

That made perfect sense to Gary. So, abandoning these seemingly empty front tents, he set off towards the rear ones, which he hoped held a few occupants.

In doing so, he went the same way that Eddie and Wanda had, just on the other side of the Big Top.

CHAPTER 25

Eddie and Wanda hadn't been walking for long before they became aware that someone was following them.

"Stop," Eddie told Wanda, holding her arm. "Do you feel what I'm feeling?"

Wanda nodded. The feeling was like gooseflesh, a chill that defied explanation.

Husband and wife were walking between two tents that opened in opposite directions, in both cases away from this thoroughfare. Their walking through here was the result of a diversion, taken after they'd noticed light spilling from the open entrance of a tent a short distance ahead on their original path.

Eddie and Wanda looked left and right, but saw no one. However, due to both of them being criminals of long experience, there was no doubt in their minds that possibly unfriendly eyes had them under surveillance.

"Let's wait and see if it's Gary," Eddie said, and then he pulled Wanda off of the aisle between the tents and into the shadows beside the one on their left.

They waited there in silence for a while, expecting the park ranger to show up. All the while, the feeling of being under surveillance persisted.

"No, it ain't Gary," Wanda said after a while. "You know, Eddie, maybe we should just go home. We can phone Ronald tomorrow to come pick up his stuff. Let's just go back to Gary, wait out his bullshit search, and drive home. Something about tonight is giving me the creeps."

Eddie nodded. "You're right. I don't like this either. Okay, gimme a minute to call Ronald, and then we'll go join up with Ranger Danger again."

Wanda smiled. "At least we can have a few laughs helping him on his wild-goose chase."

Eddie placed a phone call to Ronald. "No reply," he informed Wanda.

"Try him again. If he still doesn't pick up, send him a text message, and let's go. Better still, let's go first, and you can text him later."

Ordinarily, Eddie would have grumbled at her to stop rushing him. But he could see she was worried, frightened actually. And, though he didn't want to admit it to her, he was frightened, too.

Eddie had had similar feelings before, and heeding them had saved his life more than once. Eddie always recognized those feelings when they arrived. Once you began feeling like the world was inexplicably turning upside down, then you quit what you were up to and you got the hell out of Dodge City.

Yeah, fuck this late-night delivery! Eddie decided.

"Let's go, babe," he whispered to Wanda.

He was surprised to see that she wasn't moving.

"Hey, what's it now?" he asked her in irritation, his fear and worry starting to get the better of him. "First, you're ready to leave, and now that I'm ready to go like you're asking, you've gone cold. Make up your damn mind!"

"Eddie, turn around!" Wanda whispered in a frightened voice, with her fingernails digging into his flesh like claws.

"What the hell?" But Eddie turned around and saw what Wanda was pointing at. A short distance away, a solitary kangaroo stood watching them.

And then, even though his senses were screaming at him to grab Wanda and take off running for the circus parking lot, Eddie Bush tried to relax and joke:

"Hey, if it isn't the circus's boxing kangaroo," he laughed, walking forward towards the animal. Suddenly he felt less worried. "Hey, champ, how it's hanging?"

"No, Eddie, come back here," Wanda almost shrieked behind him, though she managed to keep her voice down, since they weren't supposed to be here at all. "Something's wrong with that animal. Look at her eyes!"

Eddie looked like she'd said, but he couldn't see any difference; the kangaroo's eyes seemed normal to him. He looked back at Wanda. "What you talking 'bout? Her eyes are normal."

Wanda gestured to him to come back to her side. "Eddie, the reason her eyes seem normal to you is because you're both standing in the shadows. I saw the kangaroo's eyes when she hopped around the corner of that tent over there. They were bright orange in color."

"What?" Eddie looked at his wife and then back at the approaching kangaroo, which had now hopped a little closer as if expecting a treat from them.

"Yeah, baby," Wanda confirmed. "I think this animal is an Agent Orange crackhead."

"Aw, you gotta be kidding," Eddie said airily.

But then it occurred to him that Wanda might be right. Eddie knew from experience that animals could become orangeheads.

He and Wanda had seen it happen once to a mouse in their house. The mouse had apparently stumbled on a dropped chunk of orange. After eating the chunk, that little mouse had then attacked and killed their cat.

The mouse had totally fucked the larger animal up, biting its way into the cat's belly and remaining inside there while the cat ran about the living room, whimpering in pain with its blood squirting everywhere.

Fuck! Eddie had almost thrown up on seeing the cat's remains. The damn crackhead mouse had still been inside of the cat at the time—it had died inside of the cat, its little head cracked open when its brain exploded like a cherry bomb.

And in this instance, we sent Ronald a package of Agent Orange . . . and Ronald trains this kangaroo. . . . Oh fuck!

Now Eddie understood that chilling feeling of nearby danger he and Wanda had gotten earlier. Animals that were strung out on 'orange' were as dangerous as human addicts. Actually, orangehead animals were more dangerous than orangehead humans, because, being animals, they lacked any human ethical programming to ponder over before they attacked and killed others.

Yeah, Wanda is right to be scared. We'd better get going now!

But then, Eddie turned around again to see that the kangaroo was flinging a punch at him. And yes, now that he was very close to it, the animal's eyes did look fucked-up.

Eddie tried to duck the boxing kangaroo's punch, but he couldn't. This was either because he was too close to the animal to evade it, or because the kangaroo simply moved too fast for him to escape her.

In any case, contact was made.

To both Eddie and Wanda's surprise, the kangaroo's punch knocked Eddie Bush's head clean off of his shoulders.

CHAPTER 26

Wanda would have screamed in terror, but she was silenced by the realization that she was currently carrying a handbag full of the most outlawed drug in the USA.

And so, she somehow, didn't begin shrieking on seeing that her husband was headless.

Eddie's decapitated corpse fell to the ground with a dull thump and squirted blood from its neck. For a while the corpse jerked on the ground, like Eddie was protesting his fate in some infernal court of the damned.

Wanda looked around for Eddie's head, but it had rolled away into the shadows and she couldn't locate it.

And now the killer kangaroo was hopping toward her. And when the kangaroo passed through a ray of light again for a second, Wanda saw that in addition to her eyes being orange, her mouth and chest were covered with blood, and blood was still dripping from her jaws.

Wanda turned and fled.

CHAPTER 27

Wanda ran with her thoughts largely garbled up by terror. She glanced back once, and saw that the kangaroo seemed to be eating pieces of Eddie's body—she was digging her claws into his chest, and when she raised her head again, she had something red that dripped with blood in her mouth.

Wanda looked forward again and almost ran into the side of a tent, one of those that didn't fit into the concentric arrangement. She caught herself just in time, and, while holding on to the side of the tent to support herself, looked back again.

What?

All of a sudden, the killer kangaroo was nowhere to be seen.

However, the mystery of where the animal had gone was quickly answered. With a loud 'thump!' the kangaroo landed three yards away from Wanda. The crazed animal's mouth and forepaws dripped blood, and here there was sufficient constant lighting for Wanda to really view the kangaroo's eyes, which projected a crazy hunger at her.

As Eddie Bush's wife, Wanda was used to seeing the eyes of drug addicts. It was common for their gaze to reveal their pathetic craving, a craving which, the more addicted they grew, often seem to replace their souls. All they had left at that later stage was hunger, an insatiable need for the needle or the crack pipe.

What Wanda felt she saw in this kangaroo's eyes was the extreme form of that emptiness of soul; a creature motivated by perverted desires and nothing more.

Wanda let out a shriek of horror and bolted again. Behind her, the kangaroo once more hopped up high into the air.

As a measure of her confusion and her terror, Wanda never made the connection between the kangaroo's pursuit of her and the packages of Agent Orange she had in her handbag. And this was why she didn't simply throw Sydney (she now recalled that as being the animal's name) her handbag and run away while the kangaroo was eating the drugs.

But no, unlike what Wanda had earlier pointed out to Gary Bentley about the relationship between drug addicts and drugs, now in her moment of crisis, she didn't make the mental linkage, that this crackhead animal might just want the crack she had on her.

This was largely due to the fact that she'd seen it EATING part of her late husband, which meant the kangaroo was HUNGRY.

So instead of throwing Sydney her handbag, Wanda kept the desired object with her and RAN.

A few seconds later, the kangaroo once again landed. This time ahead of her. Then it turned around and bared its teeth at her. They didn't seem like herbivore teeth to her.

Wanda Bush had stopped running at a sort of crossroads between the tents. She realized she now had a choice between darting left or right to escape Sydney. Seeing as the kangaroo wasn't yet leaping at her again, she used the brief respite in pursuit to desperately consider her options.

Left will take me out into the open. It's just the fields out there and I'll have no cover from this crazy animal that killed Eddie. I'm on the wrong side of the Big Top from the parking lot. Shit, Eddie, honey! If I go right, I'll still be in concealment and I'll be heading towards the parking lot.

So, still tightly clutching her handbag, Wanda ran to the right.

Once through the gap between tents, she found herself face-to-face with the canvas wall of the Big Top, which, at this point, was decorated with clown murals. She turned left again and began running along this wall, while the clown illustrations gave way first to those of animals and then a man on the high-wire.

Then Wanda looked up and saw the kangaroo sailing over the top of a tent up ahead, clearly trying to head off her escape again.

Wanda had no intention of continuing onward to meet up with the kangaroo.

She again considered running out between the tents into the open fields, but then changed her mind. The kangaroo had landed out of sight, and for the moment, it couldn't see her. She, however, had just reached one of the Big Top's side entrances.

She ducked through the tent flap and found herself in almost complete darkness.

CHAPTER 28

"What the fuck?" Cedric said on seeing Otis's corpse.

Otis lay on his left side with his back to them. With that gaping hole where his heart used to be, they could see all the way through his body, and the bone splinters poking out of the hole at them made Otis's mortal wound look like a misplaced mouth, the similarity compounded by the fact that the hole had bled profusely.

Mindy stood trembling and jabbing her finger at the dead man. "See, I wasn't lying about it. I wasn't lying."

Elaine took one look at the body and buried her face in Cedric's massive chest. "Oh, my God, Oh, my dear God!"

Cedric hugged her tightly. After making that first shocked comment, he, too, gaped in fright.

All three of them remained at a distance from the corpse. Ronald was the only one who walked over to get a closer look.

Ronald knelt down and turned Otis over. The dead man had a surprised look on his face, like he'd just opened his front door to an unexpected visitor.

Ronald turned to look up at the others.

"Where the hell is his heart?" he asked Mindy.

"I-I-I d-d-don't know! Th-th-the ka-ka-kangaroo was e-e-eating it!"

Ronald, Elaine, and Cedric looked at each other in horror.

"Eating it?" Ronald asked Mindy.

She nodded fiercely. "Yes, yes—that's the truth!" Mindy was looking from her dead lover's body to the tent entrance, with every motion of her body suggestive of her intense desire to flee again.

"It's okay," Elaine said. "I believe you."

"We all believe you," Ronald agreed. "So, what happened next?"

Mindy told them. On the way over here, no one wanted to hear what she had to say. Now, they all listened as if she was Jesus delivering the Sermon on the Mount. And the more they listened, the more alarmed they all became.

"Fuck!" Cedric said afterward. "We need to call the cops."

CHAPTER 29

So far, Gary Bentley's investigations had proven to be a complete waste of time. He'd stalked between the tents like a thief, twice ducking out of the way when he heard people heading his way.

He'd arrived at the back of the Big Top, where the animal cages were. The animals all appeared to be fast asleep.

"Alright, I admit I'm simply making a fool of myself here," he told himself aloud, as he stared over at the cages with their slumbering inhabitants. "But, just to make certain, I'm gonna walk around the Big Top's other side too, and then I'll fetch Eddie and his wife, and we're all leaving."

That was Gary Bentley's intention until about halfway around the Big Top, when he stepped into something wet. Now, it hadn't rained for several days, and everywhere else Gary had walked over tonight, the ground had been dry or, at most, slightly damp. But here, the ground felt not exactly muddy but quite sticky.

Because he was walking between the animal cages and the tent, Gary's first thought was that he'd stepped into some monkey feces; he'd heard monkeys sometimes threw their shit at people. He was holding a flashlight, but hadn't been using it because of his desire to remain undetected.

He flicked on the flashlight now and aimed it down at his shoe. He was surprised to see that he wasn't standing in monkey poop, but in some congealed blood. Startled by this, Gary trailed the beam of his flashlight sideways toward the source of the blood.

All of a sudden, he was shining his flashlight on a dead lion.

He pulled his shoe out of the blood, rubbed its sole over some nearby grass, and then hurried over towards the lions' cage. There were two other lions in there besides the dead one, but both seemed fast asleep.

Gary stared at the dead lion. Its head was crushed in a manner he'd never seen before. It looked like someone had taken a sledgehammer to the beast's head. Its skull was a fractured mess of blood and bones and brains, with one eye even dangling back over its right ear. Its lower jaw had swung sideways so that it was almost folded away out of sight. The dead animal lay in a pool of blood, which had then dripped out between the bars of the cage.

Or maybe someone used a shotgun on it. But this blood is still quite fresh, and besides that, there ain't no smell of gunpowder in the air or any sign of shotgun pellets nearby. Just this one lion with its head destroyed.

Both of the other lions seemed to be asleep. Gary knew this meant that whatever had killed this lion he was staring at had done so silently, which was even more puzzling.

For a hammer blow to wreak this level of damage, it would've awoken the other lions. A shotgun blast would have roused all of the animals caged out back here.

Gary was still puzzling on this, when a gut feeling made him look upward.

There, he'd just seen it again: a kangaroo, leaping at an impossible height over one of the far tents.

Gary had caught just a fleeting glimpse of the animal, which had already been descending when he'd looked up. Had he not earlier had a similar experience, he'd have thought he'd imagined it. But no, this time, he knew this was the real deal.

If a kangaroo can leap that high, what else can it do?

Feeling worried, he stared back down at the dead lion's head.

Can the circus's boxing kangaroo have punched this lion to death? What sort of ability would it require to do that? He sighed. *Aw, shucks! This is all coming together now. I should rather be asking: what kind of narcotic substance would give a kangaroo such powers? I can think of only one, and I'm currently here searching for evidence of its usage. And it looks like I may have found that evidence.*

Then Gary found another element that increased his suspicions. A long red smear lay on the grass. Gary knew he was clutching straws here, trying to force things in the direction of a conclusion. But the smear just might be a kangaroo's footprint. They did have very long feet.

Gary headed away from the lion's cage, walking cautiously towards the tent where he'd seen the kangaroo.

For reassurance, he tapped the gun at his waist.

He didn't pull the weapon out yet, though. He didn't want to run into one of the circus staff and scare them into calling the police.

I need to find that damn kangaroo fast, Gary thought. *And when I find it, will it really have huge orange eyes?*

CHAPTER 30

This late at night, the interior of the Big Top was dark. It took a while for Wanda's eyes to adjust to the dimness.

She'd entered the tent through one of the access routes to the center ring. Once she'd grown accustomed to seeing in there, she continued walking, past ladders for the trapeze artists, lots of dangling ropes, and several trampolines.

Like a silk thread overhead, she could just make out at the high wire. From down below here it appeared to her that anyone who attempted to walk across something that thin must be batshit crazy.

Something smacked her in the face, and she ran back in fright before she realized that it was simply a dangling rope for the monkey acts.

Soon she was right in the middle of Big Top, in the center of the circus ring, and surrounded by the tiers of 'indoor bleachers,' (with their risers cunningly constructed so as to be both collapsible and dismantlable) where the audience would be sitting if this was a performance.

Wanda got out her cell phone. *Now, who the hell do I call? The cops? No, I'd better call Eddie's bodyguard, Mo.*

Wanda dialed Mo's number, but got his voicemail. She left a voice message: "Listen, Mo, Eddie's dead, and I'm in danger. I'm at the circus! Come get me, but don't call the cops yet!"

She hung up and hoped Mo hadn't switched off his phone because he was in bed with a prostitute. *Sure, he has the night off, but . . . dammit, I can't believe that kangaroo killed Eddie. I'm a widow now!*

She'd loved Eddie, and the tears came now, in this window of peace and quiet, before she'd begin running again.

Wanda wept and wept, and it wasn't until she realized she wasn't alone in the Big Top tent that she wiped her eyes dry.

Oh, shit. The kangaroo has found me.

Wanda was sure of this, though she'd not yet seen or even heard anything strange. But it was the same as before; she'd gotten that same chilling feeling down her spine as when she and Eddie had been walking between the tents.

The light from her cell phone automatically meant she could see better in here. She turned on the cell phone's flashlight and swept the tent in its beam.

Rows of tiered grandstand seating left and right. Then she sensed movement to her left and swung the light that way, but there was nothing to see.

Next, she caught a flash of movement out of the corner of her eye on the right and swung her flashlight that way, too.

This time the flashlight shone on something. For a fraction of a second, she'd seen the kangaroo landing in the aisle between two of the riser frames.

Or did I?

Because now, it seemed as if the kangaroo was actually behind her, instead of in front of her.

Wanda swung her flashlight this way and that, sometimes thinking she'd seen the animal she was hiding from, but always finding out that she was wrong.

But I know I'm right! That addicted female beast is in here with me. She killed my Eddie, and if I had my gun with me now, I'd kill her too.

Wanda decided to run across the Big Top to its opposite exit.

From there it's a straight run to the Mercedes. I've got the car keys with me. Once I've got my gun . . . watch out, you damn animal!

So she ran, her shoes pattering loudly. She reached the exit aisle between the farther tiers of seats and paused. After looking back to ensure the kangaroo wasn't following her, she headed for the exit.

And then, five yards from the exit, the kangaroo hopped out from behind the section of tiered/grandstand seating on the left side of the exit, and headed for her.

Wanda shone her flashlight at the kangaroo's face, which made the creature hold up its forepaws to protect its eyes.

Wanda didn't wait. She climbed over the railing into the nearest row of seats, and ran. She heard a loud thump behind her and looked back. The kangaroo had bounded over onto the seats, but had landed awkwardly.

Wanda watched the animal try to right herself, with her right foot on a seat and the other one down in the gap between that seat and the back of the seat ahead of it. The kangaroo fumbled around for a while before she managed to also get her foot up onto the seat. Then, once she was properly balanced, she leapt again towards Wanda.

Wanda hurried out of range, then turned and shone her flashlight at the kangaroo again. She saw that the pursuing animal had once more landed awkwardly, once again with one leg on and one leg off of the seats.

Wanda realized that she had an advantage while she was up here between the seats. The tiered grandstand seating made it impossible for the kangaroo to balance herself. These seats on their risers were the chink in the kangaroo's armor.

So long as I remain up on the tiers, I'll be safe, she thought, *walking along her middle row of seats with careful steps. But I can't remain here forever. How can I use this to my advantage?*

Even with her life on the line here, Wanda's current situation struck her as being extremely theatrical. Here she was, inside of a giant circus tent in the dark, with the only illumination coming from her cell phone, which tenuously abraded the surrounding darkness, making it seem like the world beyond the boundaries of its weak lighting didn't exist.

At this point, it felt to Wanda almost like she was in a dramatic performance with the spotlight picking out just herself and her animal costar.

That aside, she considered her problem.

There seemed just one way to handle this:

I'll wait till the kangaroo jumps again, and then run underneath her and leap over the side railing of the stands, then out of the exit. Because she still needs to get off of the tiers first, that should give me enough of a head start to reach the car and get out my gun. Or at least to hide the drugs and then call the police to come pick up Eddie's body.

Thinking of Eddie once again upset her, and she began weeping. And it was the tears flooding from her eyes that made her not realize that the kangaroo, frustrated by her inability to land conveniently on the tiered seats, had been slowly creeping her way forward on all fours.

By the time Wanda had realized this, Sydney, the Kangaroo, was just four seats away from her.

Wanda, however, was almost completely at the end of this particular section of grandstand seats. She again trained her cellphone light on the kangaroo's eyes, which once more made Sydney hold up her paws to block out the light.

Wanda saw that she could still escape. She just needed to take two steps backward and then leap down over the railing. Or she could run down the steps beside the railing to the ground. Either approach worked, because there was an exit from the Big Top on this side of the raised seats too.

The one thing that still didn't occur to Wanda to do was to fling away her handbag before making a run for it. But then, even if she had considered doing so, she'd have rejected the thought outright. She was too conditioned to the value of Eddie's narcotics to discard them.

Keeping her cell phone flashlight trained on the kangaroo's head, Wanda took the first step back, then the second.

And then, because she wasn't looking that way at all, she lost her footing right when she was about to lever herself up and over the railing.

She slipped. As she fell, she reached for something to steady herself and managed to catch a firm grip on the railing. But her right hand, which was holding the cell phone, now struck the back of the chair beside her. That made her let go of her phone, which clattered down through the gap between the seats to land face up on the ground below.

By the rays of phone light that penetrated the gaps in the riser framework, Wanda made out the kangaroo, moving quickly over the seats towards her.

Wanda gasped, lost her footing again, and this time tumbled over the side railing to the floor.

It was a short drop, and she didn't injure herself, but for a few moments, she was stunned. She glanced over at her cell phone, which was actually within reach, though she wouldn't be able to reach it from her current position, because one of the support frames was in her way. However, if she crawled about a yard toward the exit, she could easily reach under the framework and pull her phone out.

But she never reached her cell phone, because suddenly she heard the loud thud of the kangaroo's feet as they landed mere inches from her head.

Wanda leapt up to her feet and ran. Almost like she could think as rationally as a person, the kangaroo had once again blocked off the Big Top's exit. So, Wanda ran out towards the center ring. Not caring that she was already hurting, she flung herself over the railing around the circus ring and kept going, heading for the rows of seats on the ring's other side.

CHAPTER 31

Now that the human woman was out in the open again, Sydney moved quickly.

The kangaroo clearly sensed that if the woman made it across the central ring to the tiered seats opposite, they would once again be stalemated in their game of cat-and-mouse. Sydney didn't desire this. A strange burning filled her now, a desperate craving and longing for what the fleeing human woman had in her bag.

Sydney had begun having withdrawal symptoms from her first dose of Agent Orange.

If the woman made it to the seating opposite, Sydney would once more be delayed in having the delicious orange nuts she was carrying.

So, the kangaroo leaped twice. One bound carried her all the way into the circus ring, and the other landed her right in front of the fleeing woman.

Then Sydney spun around and knocked the woman off of her feet.

The woman fell backwards, but wasn't dead. The skin on the right side of her head was split open, and her right eye had been completely pulped by the blow, but she was still alive, and she stared up at Sydney with hatred.

"You goddamn piece-of-shit-animal!" the woman spat up at Sydney, spitting so forcefully that her spit hit Sydney in the face. "If Eddie hadn't made me leave my gun in the car, I'd have fucked you up tonight."

Sydney had no idea what the woman's words meant, but she did understand the enraged tone of voice in which they were spoken. In response, she felt rage of her own, and she demonstrated her rage by leaning over the woman and punching her in the head again.

Sydney punched the woman in the head so hard that, same as had happened to her human mate, her head was completely knocked off of her shoulders. And in this case, because she'd been lying on the ground, her detached head sank about a foot into the earth, simply from the force of the blow. Then her neck leaked blood into the hole and filled it up, erasing her head from view.

***

Once the woman was dead, Sydney ripped her handbag off of its strap and got out the cache of Agent Orange. The orange 'nuts' were in several packages.

Sydney ripped one of the packages open with her claws and ate all of its contents. As the drug-filled her belly, she felt both its calming and unsettling influence mixing in her small animal mind like a smoothie. Sydney felt all was right with her world, and this meant she felt the desire to kill, kill, and kill again.

She finished up that package of Agent Orange and then opened another one.

Once this package was also empty, Sydney gathered up the remaining packages of the drug and stored them in her pouch.

Then, ignoring the dead woman with the blood-filled hole where her head used to be, Sydney hopped off out of the Big Top tent.

CHAPTER 32

"We'd better call the cops," Cedric told the others in Ronald's tent as they stood together, staring down at dead Otis by the light of a rechargeable lamp. "The police will know what to do about Sydney."

"Not yet," Ronald instantly objected. "Let's first find Sydney ourselves. Maybe we can neutralize her ourselves."

"I don't think that's gonna be possible," Mindy just as quickly said. "You didn't see that kangaroo. She was like Iron Mike Tyson on steroids!"

"Like I said, man," Cedric told Ronald with a menacing stare. "Call the fucking cops on your cell phone. Get them over here and let them deal with this mess. I don't see what your reservations are." Cedric gestured at the corpse. "We clearly didn't kill Otis."

Ronald gulped in dismay. This just got worse. *Yes, muscle-bound Cedric is right. With the way Otis died, the police won't ever prosecute any of us for his murder, not after Mindy's testimony of what had happened in here. But the problem now is, if we get the police over here before Mindy has sufficient time to calm down and think straight, her damn testimony will be sure to result in both her and me going to jail for trafficking narcotics. At the moment, neither Elaine nor Cedric know anything about our Agent Orange deals with Eddie Bush. Neither of them have any idea of what's actually wrong with Sydney—though I can hazard a guess. Roo got into the Agent Orange and is completely cracked up, fucked up in the head.*

"What the hell you waiting for, man?" Cedric angrily asked Ronald. "Dial fucking 9-1-1 already. Neither Elaine nor I have our phones on us."

94

"C'mon, dude, Just hear me out," Ronald told Cedric. "I ain't saying I won't call the police. All I'm saying is—hey, you all know how that kangaroo is to me. She's like my fucking daughter."

"Sometimes she seems more like your fucking wife," Elaine said. "If I didn't know you better, I'd think you and Sydney were having sex on a regular basis."

"Hey, that's uncalled for," Ronald said angrily. "I'm not screwing the 'roo. What I'm getting at is, gimme a chance to calm her down. I don't want the cops filling her with bullets. You all know how docile an animal Sydney is. I don't know what Otis did to her to piss her off. Maybe *he* tried to fuck her."

"He didn't try to fuck her!" Mindy yelled and flung herself at Ronald, with her fingers clenched into claws. "Your damn kangaroo just snapped and murdered him, you sleazy sonofabitch."

Ronald grabbed her hands before she scratched his face. Then he pushed her away from him, so she went down sprawling on his mattress. Mindy began weeping again.

"Okay, I'm sorry," he told Mindy. "I didn't mean it like that. I know Otis wouldn't rape my kangaroo. Now just calm down while we attempt to work this out."

"Nothing to work out," Cedric said. "Call the fucking police or gimme your phone so I can do it."

Ronald shook his head. "No, I still insist on trying to find Sydney first—"

"Stop arguing, both of you!" Elaine said, raising a hand to silence their further protests. Then she sighed. "I'm not sure which of you I agree with more. Yeah, I agree with Cedric that we should get the cops over here. But I also agree that we should try and find Sydney ourselves."

Cedric nodded. "We'll need guns, in case she attacks us, too."

"Davey has lots of guns," Elaine said, referring to the circus lion tamer. "But he's also out having fun in town tonight, and his firearms are always safely kept in a gun rack with a key, which he keeps on his person. So, how . . ." Then Elaine frowned. "Guys, one of you, please cover up Otis's body. Each time I look at him, I wanna piss myself from fright."

Mindy frowned at Elaine's statement, but didn't comment while Ronald picked up a blanket from beside her on his mattress and draped it over Otis's corpse.

"Yes, that's better," Elaine said. Then she pointed to a purple object that came rolling out of the folds of the blanket. "What the hell is that?"

The object had rolled off into a corner. Cedric walked over there and picked it up.

"We've just found Otis's missing heart," he told Elaine with a grim smile on his face, while holding the partially consumed organ up for her inspection.

With a slight gasp of fright, Elaine fainted where she stood. She slumped to the ground and lay inert with her hair covering her face and her bosom heaving fitfully.

Cedric immediately handed the dead man's half-eaten heart to Ronald. "Put it with the rest of him."

Ronald gaped at him. "Huh?"

Cedric nodded. "Yeah, you know. Stick it back in his chest or something."

Then Cedric hurried over to tend to Elaine.

Mindy began crying again.

Ronald stood there holding Otis's heart and staring at it. Contact with the organ repulsed him, but in contrast, he also felt very relaxed.

At least no one is thinking of calling the police now, he thought. *I just need to hold out until Mindy gets her act together again. Once I've coached her on what to tell the police, we'll be fine.*

CHAPTER 33

Gary Bentley's search for the kangaroo yielded no results. At one point, while walking beside the Big Top tent, he'd imagined he heard odd noises issuing from within it.

But then the supposed sounds had quickly ceased, leading Gary to conclude he'd imagined them.

He was still in two minds over whether to call the police. The lion's death might warrant such a call, but . . .

But I'd best find out what's going on first, although this is how it happens each time there's an Agent Orange crisis. First of all, it looks like nothing's wrong, and five minutes later, it's raining shit like the sky has diarrhea.

It was with those thoughts in mind that Gary peeked between two tents and saw the pair of legs. The legs, however, weren't standing upright but lay parallel to the floor.

Half of the opinion that someone had gotten drunk and fallen asleep out in the open, Gary nonetheless headed between the tents for a look, because . . .

Because this is how the rain of shit generally starts.

And then Gary found himself looking at a headless body. The man lay there with his head, nowhere to be found. Gary played his flashlight over the corpse and realized he was looking at Eddie Bush's corpse.

With a sinking feeling settling over him, Gary peeked around in confusion, shining the flashlight beam into all the nearby nooks and crannies.

But who the hell cut his head off?

Then he remembered the dead lion again.

Oh, shit, I think it's started again. And . . . and . . . where the hell is Eddie's wife, Wanda?

"Hey, Wanda!" he called out in a loud whisper. "Are you nearby?"

After about a minute of not getting any reply from Wanda Bush, Gary got out his cell phone and dialed 9-1-1.

"Hello, what is your emergency?"

"I'm forest ranger Gary Bentley. I'm at the circus—Madam Vega's Traveling Show—just outside of town . . ."

"Yes, sir, please go on."

"I've just found a headless body. A friend of mine named Eddie Bush. It looks like someone chopped his head off . . ."

"All right, sir, the police will be on their way over shortly."

CHAPTER 34

"Put that fucking thing away, man," Cedric growled at Ronald. "If she sees it and faints again, I'll . . ."

The 'fucking thing' that Cedric was referring to was Otis's heart, which Ronald still had in his hand.

Ronald nodded and lifted the blanket he'd draped over Otis's corpse. Not intending to stick his hand into the hole in Otis's chest as Cedric had suggested, Ronald dropped the dead man's heart between his arm and his body. Then he covered Otis up again.

Elaine was just coming out of her faint. In the meantime, Cedric had moved Mindy off of Ronald's mattress and moved Elaine onto it. He was sitting with her head on his lap.

Mindy was seated on Ronald's suitcase, while Ronald paced back and forth across the room.

"That was a real shock you gave me, darling," Elaine said on opening her eyes. "Totally Indiana Jones and the Temple of Doom."

"Are you okay, baby?" Cedric asked, now helping her sit up. Cedric was so muscular that Elaine looked like a doll he was holding.

She sat up, nodded, and looked around, with a look of relief entering her eyes when she saw Otis's completely covered body. "What were we going to do before I . . . ?"

"We were going to search for Sydney," Ronald said flatly.

"Yes," Elaine agreed. "We might as well go looking for the kangaroo." She made to rise to her feet and Cedric looked worried. "Hey, are you sure you shouldn't just lie down in here for a while?"

Elaine shook her head. "No, I'll be okay. It was just the shock of seeing that damn heart. Ugh, such a gruesome sight."

"Okay, so can we leave here now?" Mindy said, once Elaine was back on her feet again. "I don't know about you guys, but staring at that corpse creeps me out big time."

"Hey, calm down," Ronald told Mindy. "We'll be out of here soon. We just need to work out where to start searching."

"I ain't searching with you," Mindy said. "Nope, not me."

Suddenly, outside of the tent, the four of them heard a loud thump, like something hitting the earth. It wasn't far off either.

"What the hell was that?" Cedric asked.

"It's your damn kangaroo, Ron," Mindy said. "That's what she sounds like when she's hopping after you, leaping over tents and trailers like she's Super-Roo!"

They all listened. But the noise didn't repeat.

"That's because she's waiting," Mindy explained. "Just like she waited for me to run, I think she's waiting for all of us out there, waiting to punch out our hearts also and eat them while they're still beating."

"Stop talking crazy," Roland told her.

"Get me a drink," Elaine told Cedric. "Something to fortify me for the search ahead." Using her chin, she gestured over at Mindy. "Give her one too. Make hers a double, so she doesn't start losing it."

Cedric looked at Ronald. "What you got in here, man?"

Ronald nodded over at Mindy. "There's an unopened fifth of whiskey in the case she's sitting on."

Leaving Elaine for a moment, Cedric walked over to the suitcase and shooed Mindy off of it.

Mindy got up, spitting. "Listen, I know you think I'm exaggerating this. But you didn't get to see—"

And then there was a ripping sound overhead and Sydney crashed down through the top of the tent and landed on top of Elaine Vega, who was standing alone, right in the middle of the tent.

CHAPTER 35

What happened then was horrible, easily the most horrible occurrence of Ronald's long life.

Sydney the Kangaroo had landed *directly* on top of Elaine. And apparently, she'd dropped through the roof of the tent with the force of a crashing airplane; because, to a horrible first 'splatting' and then 'popping' noise, Elaine Vega simply crumpled and disintegrated.

First of all, she was flattened by the weight and force of the kangaroo landing right on top of her. As if she was a female tortoise retreating into her shell, Elaine's head was pushed down completely into her chest. Then, her chest and torso compressed like an accordion. And finally, the whole ridiculous compacted mess of head and torso forced itself down onto Elaine's legs, the two thigh bones of which burst their way through the top of Elaine's already squashed chest and poked out beside her head.

(This play-by-play detailed analysis of the exact nature of the circus impresario's untimely demise would only be arrived at later by Ronald, when his mind attempted to reconstruct what his eyes had witnessed at a speed too fast for his mind to comprehend.)

Of course, that kind of pressure compacting flesh and bone into spaces too small for it to occupy would produce other results, too.

In this case, Elaine Vega blew up like someone had bombed her.

Everyone present except the kangaroo was splattered with Elaine's blood and guts. The kangaroo was left standing on top of Elaine, who, to add insult to injury, had also been partly forced into the ground by the impact that had killed her.

Ronald looked at the dead woman, who now looked like something created in a mad scientist's lab; meat, flesh, and skin mangled up beyond comprehension. He peeled chunks of her flesh off of his clothes and discarded them.

Elaine's boyfriend, Cedric, stared at the kangaroo and corpse as if confused. He kept opening and shutting his mouth, blinking his eyes like he couldn't believe what they were showing him.

Mindy looked close to fainting, and her chest began heaving like she was going to throw up.

Ronald did throw up. The puke came up in an unstoppable rush. He just let the vomit out. What remained of Elaine now looked so disgusting, it would have been inhuman not to feel sick while staring at it.

Wiping his mouth afterward, Ronald suddenly realized that he'd not smoked a joint since they'd all returned to his tent. He figured he needed to smoke some marijuana right now, to help him cope with what was happening around him.

Meanwhile, Sydney was hopping back and forth beside Elaine. Squashing Elaine to death like that had wounded the kangaroo, too; the skin on the inside of her right foot was bloodily ripped open, and her tail also looked slightly skinned. But the kangaroo was still on her feet. Her pouch also bulged like she had several joeys in there.

Sydney was staring at each of them in turn, looking like she'd attack them, but also looking like she didn't intend to. Just like Mindy had already informed them, her eyes bulged a bright orange, and now had lost all definition between sclera, iris, and pupil. Squashing Elaine like a bug had increased the amount of blood on her own body; but there had clearly been a lot of it on her body to start with.

And now, Cedric's brain, frozen from the horror of what had just happened, seemed to defrost.

"Hell no, you didn't just kill Elaine, you piece of animal excrement."

And then Cedric leapt at the killer kangaroo and tackled her down to the ground.

CHAPTER 36

Used to performing feats of strength to wow and thrill circus audiences across the country, Cedric would have been more than a match for even a mountain gorilla, speak less of a kangaroo.

But this particular kangaroo had consumed a drug that had altered its entire muscular structure and had also given it, if not exactly a killer instinct, the need to kill to feel fulfilled.

Cedric and Sydney crashed down to the floor together.

At first, it seemed like Cedric had the upper hand over the kangaroo. Sydney was kicking and punching, but Cedric had gotten hold of the animal from behind, and for the most part, because he was holding her off of the ground, there was little she could do to hurt him.

But similarly, it seemed he couldn't hurt her either.

And so, rolling back and forth, Cedric and Sydney rolled and struggled their way around the floor of the tent.

But then the tide of their conflict changed. This was mostly because Cedric seemed to have no idea of how to subdue the kangaroo. He couldn't effectively hit Sydney without relinquishing control of her torso. He tried rabbit-punching her once, but that didn't work. Instead, the kangaroo bit him deeply on the arm.

The pair of them crashed around the tent some more, with Mindy leaping first over Cedric's head and then over Elaine's squashed remains, to get out of their way.

CHAPTER 37

The conflict between man and kangaroo had another, unforeseen consequence. As Cedric and Sydney struggled for ascendancy in their battle, those packages of Agent Orange that the kangaroo had stored in her pouch began spilling out onto the floor.

On noticing this windfall, Mindy couldn't believe her luck.

Wow, just look at all of this fucking orange here! For a single sad moment, she gazed regretfully over at the blanketed corpse. *Shit, Otis, baby, you up and died before the big one!*

Then the 'orangehead' in Mindy Lane came completely to the forefront, and she forgot all about her dead lover, her dead employer, and the killer kangaroo that was battling her friend. All that mattered to Mindy now was to amass the spilled drug packages for herself.

And so, completely ignoring the conflict in the tent, Mindy ducked down on the floor of the tent and began gathering up the drug packages. There were quite a lot of them. After Mindy had collected six of them, she broke one open and stuffed her mouth with the orange 'candy' it contained.

Her mind quickly exploded with impressions of both ecstasy and rage. Now, far from viewing the kangaroo as the benevolent provider of the Agent Orange, Mindy Lane began viewing the animal as a competitor.

Sydney and Cedric crashed into Rodney's suitcase, and more Agent Orange spilled from Sydney's pouch, and Mindy gathered it all up.

Finders keepers, losers weepers, she thought. The drug was hers. All hers. Hers and hers alone.

CHAPTER 38

Ronald sighed as he watched Mindy gather up the spilled Agent Orange.

At least I don't need to worry anymore about her keeping her head when the cops get here, he realized in disgust. *Damn junkie bitch has already forgotten about Otis and Elaine.*

Ronald really didn't get how people could let themselves become so reliant on narcotics that they couldn't function normally without them. Yes, he used a lot of marijuana himself, but it wasn't like his religion. But Mindy . . . Mindy now had the look of a crazed bitch about her, and that wasn't even counting the color of her eyes, which after, she'd eaten almost half a package of the Agent Orange in one sitting, had suddenly brightened up like orange light bulbs.

She doesn't seem to realize anymore that Cedric isn't wrestling this kangaroo in the WWE but is involved in a life-and-death struggle.

"Hey, give me a hand!" Cedric called out to Ronald from down on the floor of the tent. "Hit the bitch with something!"

Ronald thought Cedric seemed to be weakening. But the kangaroo he was tangling with clearly wasn't. In fact, Sydney looked enraged that Mindy was eating up the Agent Orange, and her rage was intensifying her attempt to break free from Cedric. She twisted in his grasp and slashed at him with her claws. Cedric barely missing having his nose slashed to pieces.

Cedric really looked exhausted now.

Ronald looked around, and then he remembered the knife he'd earlier stuck in his belt. The knife still hung there, forgotten amidst all the craziness.

Ronald pulled out the knife and headed for Sydney.

But how the hell am I gonna get the knife to Cedric? He's holding onto Sydney with both hands so he can't take it from me. And . . . there's no way that I'm about to go near those kicking and flailing limbs of hers. Those claws of hers are so sharp she could disembowel me without even trying!

But the conflict had ended almost before he'd reached the kangaroo. She and Cedric's last roll through the tent, had wound up slamming Cedric's head against Elaine's corpse. The shock of the impact made Cedric loosen his grip on Sydney's midriff.

Before Cedric could regain his hold of Sydney, the kangaroo had freed herself from his grasp, for good this time.

She lashed at Cedric with her forepaws.

Cedric safely rolled out of the way of the slashes, but now wound up rolling into Otis's body.

He spun around and tried to get up, but Sydney was already hopping on top of him, with her claws flashing at his face.

Cedric screamed. When Sydney hopped out of the way for an instant, Ronald saw why. Sydney had ripped Cedric's face completely off of his skull with her claws. Cedric still had both of his eyes, but the left one was completely shredded to goo.

Sydney, meanwhile, slowly ate Cedric's removed face.

Even though he was now faceless and half-blind, Cedric still attempted to rise to his feet and take on the kangaroo, but Sydney shoved him back down and now began punching his head with her forepaws. She hit him exactly the way Ronald had trained her to fight—left, right, left, right . . . pause and duck, then left uppercut, right uppercut.

She was punching Cedric's head against Otis's corpse, and the result was ruinous to both bodies.

Essentially, by the time the kangaroo was done, she had punched Cedric's head into Otis's torso through the blanket. Cedric lay dead on the ground with his head completely inside of the other man's body.

Ronald didn't think there would be much left of Cedric's head either.

He noticed that Sydney was staring at him, with blood dripping down her body. Her forepaws now dripped a pinkish pulp that Ronald assumed was composed mostly of Cedric's brains.

For the moment, at least, the kangaroo seemed to recognize him. She seemed to understand that she was at home here; and that he wasn't a threat to her.

Ronald wondered how long that would last.

But he wouldn't find out yet, because now Sydney had turned her attention away from him and was staring angrily at Mindy, who, seemingly oblivious to Cedric's death, was now engaged in popping an orange nugget into her mouth.

CHAPTER 39

"You know what I'm thinking?" Mindy asked Ronald. "I'm thinking this has to be the orange that Eddie Bush wanted Otis and me to deliver to that guy Cutthroat Kelly in Elkins . . . 'cos Eddie was supposed to bring it here tonight. But if he was, then how did Sydney get the fucking drugs?"

On hearing her name called, Sydney hissed at Mindy.

"Back the fuck off, bitch!" Mindy hissed back at the kangaroo and snatched the gathered Agent Orange off of the ground before the kangaroo could reach it.

Here comes another bloody death, Ronald thought. *Mindy's gathered up all of the orange crack in the room, and now the pair of them are going to duel to the death for it. Aw well. Goodbye, Mindy, it's been real nice knowing you!*

"Hey, just give her the Agent Orange!" he called out to Mindy.

"Stay the hell out of this!" Mindy yelled back. "This is between me and Miss Furry Longtail here!"

Ronald nodded. "Have it your way. Just don't blame me when she kills you too."

"That ain't gonna happen, Ron."

In all honesty, Ronald wasn't overly concerned about Mindy's survival in this anticipated contest. In his own current drug-related situation, Mindy was clearly the weakest link.

If she dies as a result of her own stupidity, all of my police worries will automatically be over. I'll be completely in the clear. She's clearly an orangehead. The cops won't even attempt to associate me with Sydney's manic and violent behavior.

Moving carefully around the corpses in his way, Ronald sidled over to where he kept his stash of pot and got out a half-smoked joint. After lighting up, he headed back to where he'd been standing and resumed watching the strange contest of wills now occurring between young woman and female kangaroo.

Even in this current surreal situation, with three crazily-fucked-up corpses in the tent, this standoff between Sydney and Mindy counted as one of the weirdest things Ronald Reed had ever witnessed.

Sidney and Mindy seemed to be staring each other down. Ronald expected them to burst into violence against one another at any moment, but weirdly, that wasn't happening. It was as odd a situation as setting matches to gasoline and seeing nothing happen.

CHAPTER 40

Mindy stared down the kangaroo. It wanted the drugs; she had the drugs, and wasn't about handing them over.

Of course, no vocal communication was possible between them, but the pair seemed to understand themselves on a psychic level, as if their shared addiction formed a bridge between them.

By now, both of these females had eyes of such orange brilliance that they could have been twin sisters.

On this Agent Orange plane, only the drug existed. Only the orange nuggets in Mindy's possession had significance. Otis, Elaine, and Cedric's corpses might never have existed. Ronald was less than a figment of their imagination. All was the drug; all had to be the drug.

Agent Orange was both God and King.

And so, Mindy and the kangaroo stared each other down. Each recognized the other as a kindred soul, a worshipper in this temple of the drug-addicted. Each also understood that there were others, those not of this addicted and damned flock, infidels who needed to be eliminated, so that only the true worshippers, only those who understood the importance of Agent Orange, could dominate the present situation, so that Sydney and Mindy alone could peacefully consume the supply of the drug that they had.

This understanding passed between them like a computer virus, infected information transmitting from one manically morphed mentality to another.

Finally, Mindy nodded. Then she lobbed a chunk of Agent Orange at Sydney.

The kangaroo snapped the chunk out of the air with bloody teeth. Mindy threw her another one, and she snapped this up, too.

Mindy smiled. "You go kill the infidels, girl," she told the kangaroo. "I'll watch over our stash. And when this is through, we'll split it up between us."

And then the spell of chemical magic was broken. The outside world came into existence again for these two crazy creatures.

And then Sydney turned and hissed at Ronald and hopped towards him. He was, after all, one of those non-believers in Agent Orange.

CHAPTER 41

Ronald regarded the approaching kangaroo through something of a marijuana haze.

If the fact that he'd begun smoking had enabled him to understand what was transpiring between woman and kangaroo, it had also clouded one major fact: that he was considered one of the infidels to be eliminated.

But, once Sydney was two yards away from him, Ronald's mind cleared away the mental haze sufficiently to focus on his survival.

Maybe the marijuana he was smoking helped enhance the imagery, but at the moment, his pet kangaroo looked more like a giant ruby statue than a mammal; that was how covered in blood Sydney was, blood that had both painted her fur crimson and then matted it down into a glossy slick surface that reflected light. In places, the blood was layered on itself, creating fake blackish stripes.

Rodney stared at her in horrified fascination. Even with the corpses in the room, and having witnessed the brutal creation of two of them, Ronald still had difficulty reconciling the past animal with the present one.

"Whoa, girl," Ronald told Sydney, as she assumed the boxing stance he'd taught her. "Take it easy now, girl. I'm on your side."

The kangaroo hopped on the spot, but made no attempt to attack Ronald.

"Yeah, that's right," Ronald told her in a tone intended to calm her down. "We're together, Sydney. Me and you, just like always."

At first, Ronald thought his soothing speech was calming the kangaroo, but then she looked back at Mindy, and Mindy shook her head at her.

"No, he ain't one of us," Mindy told Sydney with a cold smile. "We don't need him anymore."

That seemed to confirm Ronald's fate. Sydney spun around and leapt at Ronald, her feet kicking out at him.

Roland may have been slightly mellow from smoking pot, but his reflexes, reflexes conditioned from years of both training Sydney and in-ring performance with her, saved him. He stepped cleanly out of the way before the kangaroo disemboweled him. Then, knowing he needed an advantage if he was to survive this assault, Ronald leapt over the corpses on the floor and retrieved the knife he'd left on the table across the tent when he'd gotten out his joint.

He spun around to see Sydney coming at him again. Once more, he successfully dodged her deadly flying feet. And this time, as she went past him, he stuck the knife in her. He'd aimed for her belly but missed, and the blade instead sliced Sydney's pouch open all the way down, leading to both a blood spill and a spilling of another two packages of Agent Orange.

The kangaroo squealed loudly. She was hurt, but not mortally. She twisted in pain, and Ronald almost lost his hold of the bloody knife as it cut her pouch open.

Ronald didn't hang around. He knew that now that he'd wounded the kangaroo, she'd be even more intent on killing him than she'd been before.

Knife in hand, Ronald fled. At the door of his tent, he turned around to see Mindy picking up the two spilled packages of Agent Orange off of the floor and then fishing around in the kangaroo's torn pouch for more while Sydney licked her wound.

Crazy, just crazy, Ronald thought and ran out into the night.

"Go get him, Sydney," he heard Mindy say behind him. "Don't let that stabbing sonofabitch get away!"

CHAPTER 42

Gary Bentley had finally located Eddie Bush's severed head. The head was beneath tent fabric, trapped and held in place by a guy rope.

Gary shone his flashlight on Eddie's head. "Sorry, man," he said, now in even greater horror than he'd felt on discovering Eddie's decapitated body.

This was because Eddie's head had a hole in its left side, one so deep that it seemed to reach almost all the way through it. Shining the flashlight beam into the hole revealed Eddie's left ear deep inside his head.

Gary flicked off the flashlight and shuddered at the brutality of the wound.

What the hell kind of crazy strength is needed to punch a guy like this? For sure, forensics are gonna have a field day with this one.

Then he heard the scream. Then the noise was gone. Then he heard a second scream.

Oh shit! It's happening again!

With his view obstructed by the tent in front of him, he couldn't pinpoint the exact location of the noise, but he knew it was somewhere on his right.

He listened again, but there were no further screams.

He pulled out his gun, looked at it, and shook his head.

I really should just let the cops deal with this, he thought. *I've called them, and they must be on their way by now. But . . . dammit . . . how many other corpses are they likely to find here if I don't get over there now?*

Gary cautiously headed in the direction the screaming had come from. A light came on in the first tent he stepped towards, and then a man poked out his head through the tent entrance.

"What's going on, man?" the man asked on seeing Gary, his eyes widening when he saw the gun in Gary's hand. "Who are you? What are you doing here at this time of night?"

"I'm not the problem," Gary told the man. "If you wanna help, call the cops. I already called them, but call them again, and tell them to get their asses over here pronto. And after you're done calling the police, don't you dare come out of your tent again, no matter what you hear. Stay indoors till you hear the police sirens."

The man nodded and ducked back inside his tent.

Gary moved on past the tent.

CHAPTER 43

Ronald kept on running, heading for the tents. He looked back, didn't see Sydney, and kept on going. Then he pulled up to a sharp halt. He'd just seen Sydney leaping over a tent. From her trajectory, she was heading forward to cut him off.

He looked at the bloody knife in his hand. He hadn't wanted to attack the kangaroo, but the beast was dangerous. And now that she'd teamed up with crackhead Mindy, she was maybe four times as dangerous.

Thanking Mindy for sharing the details of her earlier flight from Sydney, Ronald ducked around the edge of the next tent to avoid the kangaroo.

He was moving so fast that although he noticed the man lying on the ground in his path, he had no time to get out of the way. He attempted to leap over the body, which to his horror, he now noticed was headless, but though his front foot easily cleared the body, his rear foot didn't. So, he tripped and went flying through the air.

Ronald hit the ground hard and was knocked out.

CHAPTER 44

Gary Bentley ran into the tent the screaming appeared to have originated from.

A single look around confirmed to him that he was in the right place. The tent contained three corpses in crazy states of death and a young woman with bright orange eyes.

"Where the hell is the killer kangaroo?" he demanded of the girl with bright orange eyes.

The young woman laughed, popped a chunk of Agent Orange into her mouth, and, while chewing it like gum, pointed vaguely around.

"Oh, Sydney?" she asked. "Sydney just hopped out to kill her trainer. You'll need to look for her, but she's definitely out there somewhere, murdering Ronald. I doubt you'll be in time to save the sonofabitch."

Gary turned around and raced back out of the tent again.

CHAPTER 45

Ronald soon revived. Still stunned from his fall, but knowing he needed to resume his flight, he staggered to his feet. He looked around for his knife, and saw it by the headless man's left foot. The sight of the decapitated corpse merely increased his terror.

He started to go pick the knife up. But then, a loud and resounding 'thump!' on the ground behind him announced Sydney's arrival.

Ronald turned around slowly. "No, Sydney, we're friends," he told the kangaroo as she leapt through the air at him. "I'm sorry I stabbed you."

But Sydney was already kicking at him. Ronald howled as the kangaroo's legs punctured all the way through his belly.

Bleeding a river, he fell to his knees while the kangaroo leapt away from him.

Despite the magnitude of his wounds Ronald wasn't dead yet, which was unfortunate for him, as it meant he felt all of the agony, when Sydney leapt forward again and kicked bloody holes in his chest.

CHAPTER 46

Gary had hardly exited the tent with the crack-addicted girl in it when he heard a man scream.

Flashlight in left hand, pistol in right hand, Gary ran in the direction of the scream, which led back up the way he'd come, to where he'd left Eddie Bush's body.

When he got there, he discovered he was too late to help the fresh victim, who lay in a pool of blood with his shirt punched full of holes.

The killer kangaroo was bent over the dead man and ripping flesh from his chest.

Gary shone his flashlight on Sydney the kangaroo, who now turned to face him also. She, too, was wounded; her pouch hung all the way open and dripped blood. In a testament to the night's murderous activity, Sydney's entire body appeared to be soaked in blood; at least her front parts clearly were.

This is bad. Real bad, Gary thought. *This makes at least five people this kangaroo has killed tonight. No, make that number SIX—I still haven't found Wanda, and she seemed to stick to Eddie like glue. Then there's also the dead lion.*

Gary kept the flashlight shining on the kangaroo. The glare made her eyes glow brightly as she ate the bleeding human flesh that was in her mouth. She lifted her forepaws to block out the light.

Cursing Max Carillo, the dead chemist who'd invented Agent Orange for perhaps the thousandth time, Gary raised his gun and sighted it on the kangaroo.

He fired, but Sydney was already leaping at him, and because he had to get out of her way, the shot went slightly wide. Still, the bullet hit the kangaroo somewhere on her left flank as she went past. Gary was sure of that.

He'd fallen sideways onto a tent and quickly hurried to right himself again because now, he knew the kangaroo was already bounding at him again. He'd heard her land, and seemed to have heard her muscles uncoil like springs to once more fling her towards him.

He turned around as quickly as he could. The kangaroo was almost on top of him and so this time he fired wildly, the bullet zipping off into the night.

He'd ducked again while shooting, but not fast enough. As Sydney passed over him, her left foot crashed against his right arm, and his arm broke. Gary heard the bones snap in his forearm, and then felt the rush of pain to his head.

The pain made him dizzy, and he dropped his gun and staggered backward, which ended up with him falling backward over the newly-dead man, whom the crackhead girl in the tent had earlier identified as being Sydney's trainer.

Gary hit the ground much harder than he'd have liked to. He did, however, manage to keep his head up. He wasn't stunned, but had had the wind knocked out of him.

Broken forearm or not, he rolled over and shone the beam of the flashlight, which he'd managed to hold on to, around in the space between the tents, trying to locate his gun.

He quickly found his gun. The crackhead kangaroo was standing on it.

Gary groaned and played his flashlight beam over the animal, which was standing three yards away and baring its teeth at him. Sydney was bleeding from where he'd shot her, but since she had been covered in blood to begin with, Gary found it impossible to identify the wound from her general crimson state.

I'm about to go extinct in like five to ten seconds, if I don't do something right now, Gary thought, looking desperately round for a weapon that would be effective against the kangaroo.

He soon located a bloody knife four feet away, and tried to drag himself towards it. In between glances at Sydney, who strangely now seemed to be relishing his pain, Gary pulled himself on towards the knife, feeling his back grow wet and sticky from the dead kangaroo trainer's blood.

After placing his flashlight on Eddie's body and angling it towards Sydney, he grabbed the knife.

When he picked the knife up, he felt a little bit better. He wasn't unarmed any longer.

But . . . how the hell am I gonna use this weapon? This bitch kangaroo broke my right arm, and I'm right-handed. I can't stab her with my left arm and hold the flashlight on her at the same time.

Then the kangaroo bounded through the air and landed directly on top of his unbroken arm. The knife sailed away into the night and Gary screamed as his remaining good arm broke also.

The kangaroo had meanwhile hopped back to where she'd initially leapt from.

Gary fought through the waves of agony, trying his best to remain conscious, because he knew that if he gave into unconsciousness, he wouldn't be able to defend himself against this manmade monster mutant mammal.

He managed to avert his fainting crisis, even though the pain in his two broken arms was terrible. Bones were sticking out of his newly fractured left forearm up near the elbow.

Gary gazed up at the kangaroo. Fortuitously, his flashlight was now pointing directly at her. Gary began counting down his life expectancy.

Maybe I hurt her worse than I thought with that gunshot. But wounded animals are often more dangerous than—

And that was how far he got with his thoughts before something unexpected happened.

Moving almost as fast as Sydney had been, a human silhouette rushed towards them.

Gary had just realized that this was the crack-addicted girl from the tent with the dead bodies when the young lady quickly wrapped her hands around Sydney's neck, and with a massive twist to the right, broke the kangaroo's neck. The sound of the kangaroo's neck bones snapping was as loud as the noise of Gary's arm bones breaking had been.

And just like that, it was all over. Sydney the kangaroo crashed to the floor dead.

CHAPTER 47

"Thanks for saving my bacon," Gary whispered up at the young lady, who stood poised in the flashlight spotlight. "A few seconds later and I'd have been a goner."

"I didn't do it for you," she said harshly while stepping over the dead animal to get nearer to him. "I did it 'cos this stupid bitch animal stole our drugs and then killed my boyfriend. And now she was gonna steal the new batch of drugs we'd ordered."

After saying this, she first turned back and kicked the kangaroo in anger, then she dug her hand into her right pants pocket and pulled out two orange chunks and flung them into her mouth. Once again, she began chewing the narcotic like gum.

"That's alright," Gary said with a sigh. "Sometimes the thought doesn't count, just the action."

The young woman nodded. Gary winced as he looked at her.

Did her eyes just brighten up even more?

She had a completely manic look on her face, like she wasn't completely done with her violence. He began hoping that she wouldn't kill him too, just because doing so would make her feel happy.

"You okay, man?" the young woman asked in a concerned voice. "You look pretty busted up."

"I'll be okay," Gary said. "Hey, thanks again. What's your name?"

"Mindy Lane. Alright, I'd better go call you an ambulance. I left my phone in the tent."

But then Mindy began jerking about like a puppet. Then, she sank down on her knees by Gary's side, and while he watched in horror, her head split wide open and her brains popped out like popcorn.

Mindy Lane's brains were a brilliant orange color. Agent Orange addict brains.

The dead young woman finally fell sideways on top of Gary. He, of course, was unable to push her off of him.

This is the craziest night of my life, Gary thought. *Not to mention the most painful. I got two broken arms and a dead crack-addict is lying on top of me. And I'm lying on the grass in a pool of someone else's blood, in the company of two dead men and a dead crackhead kangaroo.*

But at least help was on the way. In the background, out beyond the tents, Gary Bentley could now hear police sirens arriving at Madam Vega's Traveling Show.

The End

ABOUT THE AUTHOR

Gary Lee Vincent was born in Clarksburg, West Virginia, and is an accomplished author, musician, actor, producer, director, and entrepreneur. In 2010, his horror novel *Darkened Hills* was selected as 2010 Book of the Year winner by *Foreword Reviews Magazine* and became the pilot novel for *DARKENED - THE WEST VIRGINIA VAMPIRE SERIES*, which encompasses the novels *Darkened Hills, Darkened Hollows, Darkened Waters, Darkened Souls, Darkened Minds* and *Darkened Destinies*.

He has also authored the bizarro thriller *Passageway,* a tribute to H.P. Lovecraft, *When the Bedposts Shake*, an erotic horror, *THE BLACK CIRCLE CHRONICLES,* a five-part mini-series that includes the books *Prove Your Love, Strange New Powers, Night Wings, Sheep Amongst Wolves,* and *Lord of the Birds,* and the *CRACKIMALS* series of horror-comedies (featuring titles *Crackcoon, Crackodile, Cracksquatch, Crackroaches, Crackadillo,* and *Crackaroo*) in association with Director Brad Twigg and screenwriter Todd Martin of Fuzzy Monkey Films, who is doing their film counterparts.

Gary co-authored the novel *Belly Timber* with John Russo, Solon Tsangaras, Dustin Kay, and Ken Wallace and *Attack of the Melonheads* with Bob Gray and Solon Tsangaras.

As an actor, Gary has appeared in over a hundred feature films, including *Prove Your Love, Faded Memories, Midnight,* and *My Uncle John is a Zombie,* and multiple television series, including *House of Cards, Mindhunter, The Walking Dead,* and *Stranger Things.* You can also find Gary in the motion picture adaptation of *Crackcoon,* playing Jonathan, the forest ranger.

Gary made his directorial debut with *A Promise to Astrid.* He has also directed the films *Desk Clerk, Dispatched, Midnight, Godsend, Strange Friends,* and *Shoulder Down: Road to Redemption.*

OTHER GREAT TITLES FROM

WWW.BURNINGBULBPUBLISHING.COM

GARY LEE VINCENT

PASSAGEWAY

GARY LEE VINCENT'S
DARKENED
THE WEST VIRGINIA VAMPIRE SERIES

DARKENED HILLS

When evil descends on a small West Virginia town, who will survive?

Jonathan did not start out his life to become a rambler, it just worked out that way. William was a troubled youth with something to hide. Both were from Melas, a small town tucked away in the West Virginia hills... a town where disappearances are happening more and more frequently.

After the suicide of a wanted serial killer, the townsfolk thought the nightmare was over. But when a centuries-old vampire is discovered they find out the hard way it's just getting started. Dark secrets can only stay hidden for so long and when the devil comes to collect, there will be hell to pay. Can Jonathan and William find a way to stop the vampire before it's too late? Find out in *Darkened Hills*!

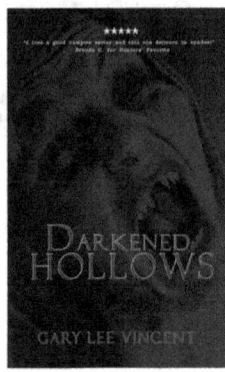

DARKENED HOLLOWS

In the heart-stopping sequel to the award-winning *Darkened Hills*, Jonathan and William must return to West Virginia to face possible criminal charges stemming from their last visit to the damned town of Melas, where both had narrowly escaped the clutches of a vampire seethe.

And as livestock start mysteriously getting murdered with all of their blood drained, worried farmers are searching for answers - leaving the local Sheriff and his deputy racing against time to learn the cause before a more violent crime is committed.

Burning Bulb

WWW.DARKENEDHILLS.COM

GARY LEE VINCENT'S
DARKENED
THE WEST VIRGINIA VAMPIRE SERIES

DARKENED WATERS

When the world goes to hell, the chosen must arise!

As Talman Cane orchestrates a flood of epic proportions in this third installment of the *Darkened* series the towns of Melas and Tarklin are caught completely off guard by the deluge. Hell-bent on finishing what they started, the evil brothers return to the lunatic asylum to take care of the witnesses and add to the ever-growing army of the undead.

Aided by Lucifer himself and the insane vampire demon Legion, the stage is set to channel all of the forces of hell to come forth. In an all-out race to survive, Jonathan, William, and Amanda soon discover they are up against impossible odds as Lucifer opens the Gateway to Hell, ushering in the zombie apocalypse and the End Times.

Find out who will survive this cosmic battle of the ages in *Darkened Waters*!

DARKENED SOULS

Melas and the Madison House are about to be rebuilt.
True evil is about to be reborne!

Young ex-priest and vampire-killer William is drawn back to the West Virginian town that almost killed him, where his vampire arch-enemy Victor Rothenstein still stalks the earth.

The town of Melas lies destroyed after the battle of the End of Days. But why is wealthy Jackie Nixon so eager to rebuild it using the bone dust of murdered souls?

Terrible evil has visited before, but the Gateway to Hell is about to be reopened in a horrific climax. And this time – it's personal.

WWW.DARKENEDHILLS.COM

Burning Bulb

GARY LEE VINCENT'S
DARKENED
THE WEST VIRGINIA VAMPIRE SERIES

DARKENED MINDS

Jackie Nixon intends to become Vampire Queen, but at what blood-drenched cost?

In this continuation to the explosive infernal saga begun in Darkened Souls, newly turned vampire Jackie Nixon is taking no prisoners. Accompanied by her daughter, Kate, and by the captive vampire lord Victor Rothenstein, Jackie Nixon explores the Darkness. There, she intends to rouse the slumbering vampire race, bound under an ancient curse, and with their help, rule the human world.

But there's a deadly threat to Jackie's plans. Not just William who is trying to stop her, but her own royal ambitions. If Jackie performs the ritual to wake the sleeping vampires the wrong way, she could instead free the Red Beast of Hell, an unspeakable evil that even the undead fear.

DARKENED DESTINIES

With over 45 people missing after Jackie Nixon's party, the mysteries surrounding Melas and the Madison House keep getting darker.

Now, with legions of vampires at her command, can anything or anyone stop her from gaining complete control over all mankind?

The final battle has begun! As the Vampire Queen ascends her throne and sets to unleash the full forces of darkness, the fate of all things good hangs in the balance.

Burning Bulb

www.DARKENEDHILLS.com

WHEN THE BEDPOSTS SHAKE

An Erotic Terror

GARY LEE VINCENT

STRANGE
FRIENDS

GARY LEE VINCENT

PROVE YOUR
LOVE

GARY LEE VINCENT

STRANGE NEW
POWERS

THE BLACK CIRCLE CHRONICLES - BOOK 2

GARY LEE VINCENT

NIGHT
WINGS

THE BLACK CIRCLE CHRONICLES - BOOK 3

GARY LEE VINCENT

SHEEP AMONGST
WOLVES

THE BLACK CIRCLE CHRONICLES - BOOK 4

GARY LEE VINCENT

LORD OF THE
BIRDS

THE BLACK CIRCLE CHRONICLES - BOOK 5

GARY LEE VINCENT

RIVER
A VAMPIRE'S NIGHTMARE

GARY LEE VINCENT

A Vampire's Nightmare Continues . . .

RIVER

Book 2 ICARUS

GARY LEE VINCENT

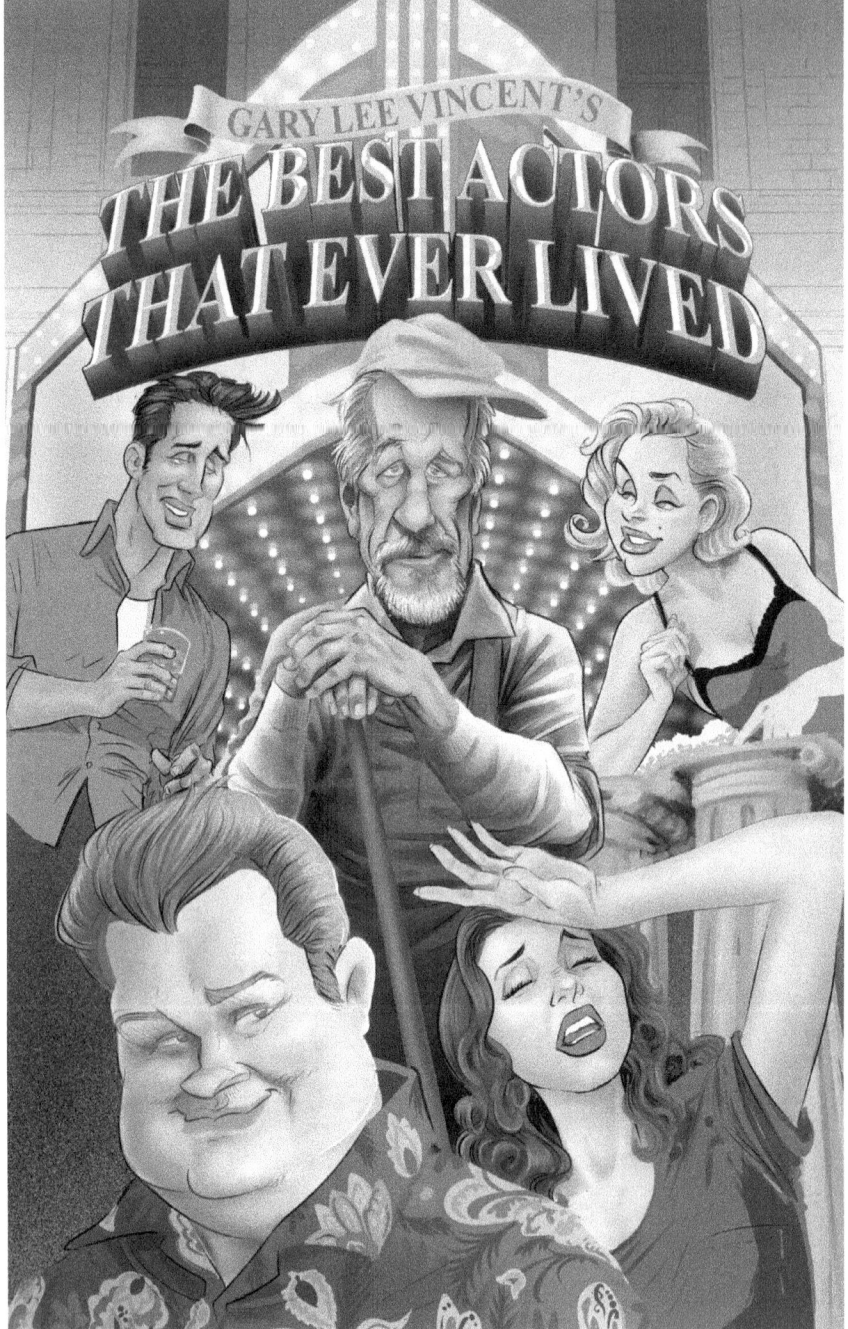

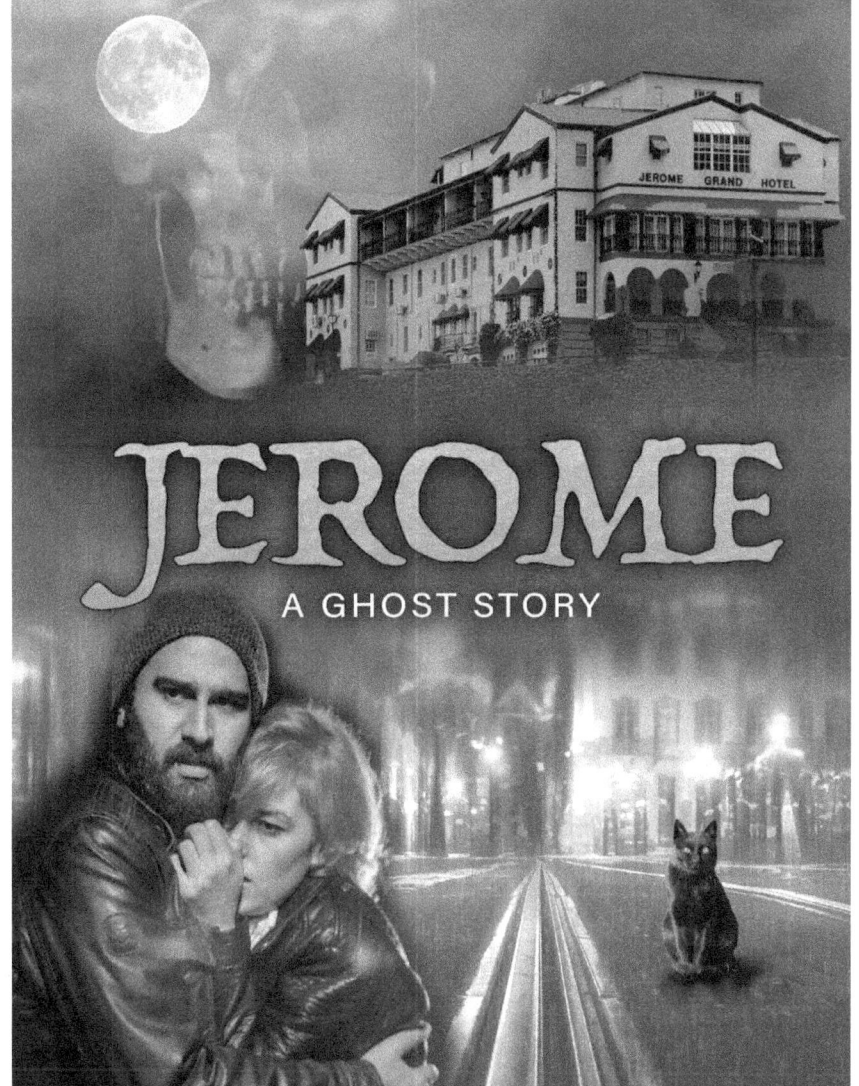

JEROME
A GHOST STORY

GARY LEE VINCENT

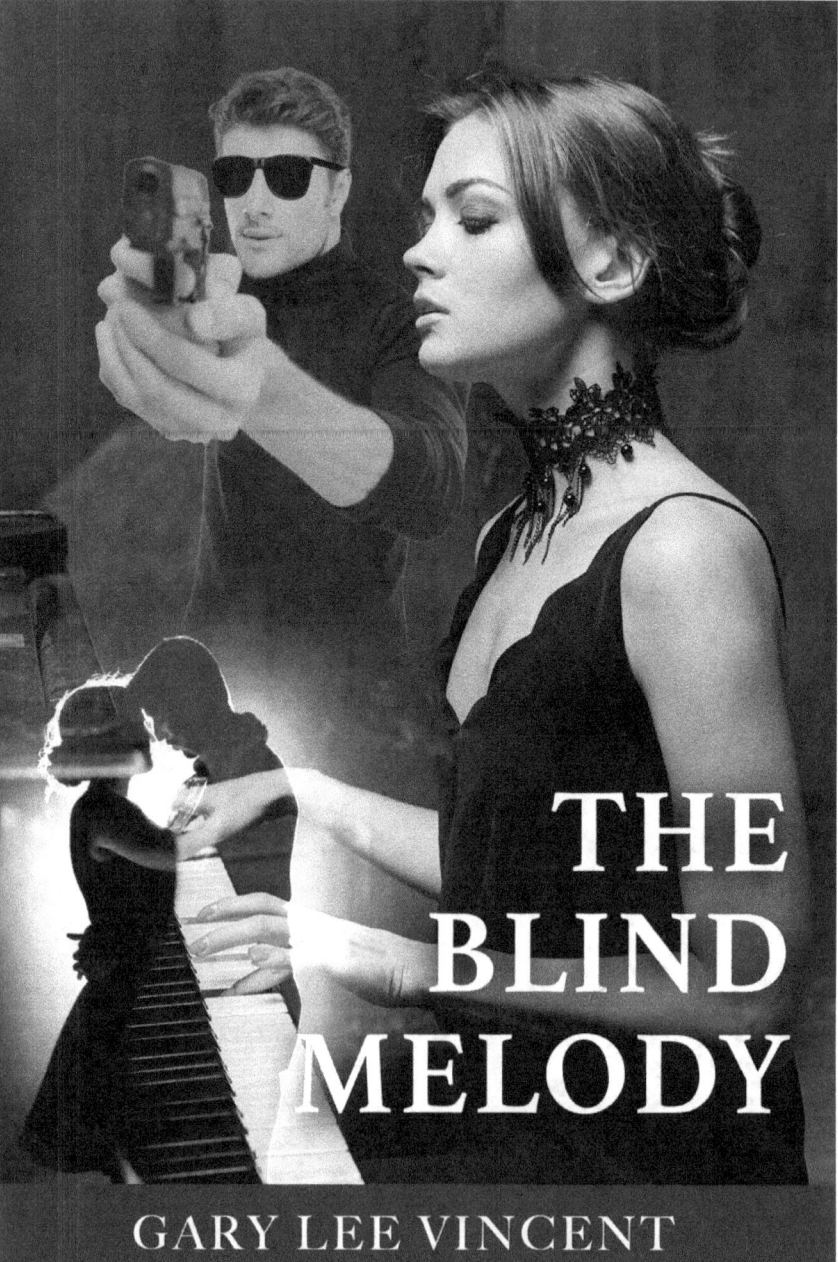

THE
BLIND
MELODY

GARY LEE VINCENT

RISE OF THE DEAD

AN EARTH-SHATTERING ANTHOLOGY OF ZOMBIE TERROR

Featuring Stories By:

John A. Russo   Tyson Blue   E.L. Stice   Nelson W. Pyles
Andy Rausch   Stephen Spignesi   R.D. Riley   Zakary McGaha
David J. Fairhead   Gary Lee Vincent   David C. Hayes   Rachel Montgomery
Paul Victor Wargelin   David F. Walker   William Vitka
Rich Bottles Jr.   Douglas Brode

Also, check out **CRACKCOON**, the motion picture from
Director Brad Twigg -- www.CrackcoonFilm.com

www.ingramcontent.com/pod-product-compliance
Lightning Source LLC
Chambersburg PA
CBHW070937250626
47159CB00009B/3280